SLAY BELLS RINGING

A MURDER MYSTERY DUET

EMILY JAMES

STRONGHOLD BOOKS

Editor: Christopher Saylor at www.sayloredting.wordpress.com/services/

Cover Design: Steven Novak at www.novakillustration.com

Published January 2019 by Stronghold Books

CONTENTS

UNSILENT NIGHTS

A MAPLE SYRUP MYSTERY NOVELLA

CHAPTER 1

When I promised to stick by Mark in sickness and in health, I hadn't thought the sickness part would come so soon. We hadn't even been married a week.

The thermometer I'd bought in the cruise ship's pharmacy beeped.

I retrieved it from Mark's mouth. "You don't have a fever, so it's not the flu."

"Maybe food poisoning." Mark's voice had a rough quality to it. Neither of us had slept much last night.

Food poisoning didn't seem likely to me. The cruise line we'd selected for our honeymoon had excellent ratings and reviews. None had mentioned food poisoning.

There was always a first time. We'd already crossed seasickness off the list. Mark had no problem when we'd been out on my parents' boat over the summer.

He closed his eyes.

I brushed his hair back off his forehead. This wasn't how we'd wanted our honeymoon to go, but we had our whole lives together. This wouldn't be the last time one of us got sick. Ten years from now, it might even make for a good story to tell. "Would you like me to order room service instead of going down to the dining room?"

Mark's face took on a pinched expression. "No food."

I eased off the bed, trying not to jostle him. "I'll be as quick as I can, and I'll bring back some ginger ale. You shouldn't have any anti-nausea meds if it's food poisoning."

Mark gave a single nod.

I felt like a horrible wife leaving him, but the thought of food clearly made him feel worse. I wouldn't be any better of a wife for eating around him.

At least I didn't think so. I didn't have much in the way of role models to work from. While my parents had a happy marriage, my dad considered getting sick to be a moral failing. As a child, he sent me to school even if I was running a fever of a hundred and was throwing up. *Nurturing* wasn't exactly some-thing my parents did.

When it came to being a supportive spouse, I'd have to figure out a lot of it on my own. I hurried as fast as I could in flip flops down to the dining room. I'd be just in time for our assigned dinner time.

I stepped from the corridor into the dining room, and my brain struggled with the switch even though I'd been here multiple times. We'd picked a cruise to South America for the warm weather and Mayan temples, but with Christmas fast approaching, the dining room had been decked out in a winter wonderland theme.

Two tall Christmas trees, filled with tinsel, multi-colored lights, and glittering gold, green, and red balls, flanked the stage. Giant snowflakes hung from the ceiling in lines leading to the central chandelier, and Christmas music played softly in the background.

While I knew that many parts of the world did have warm weather for Christmas, growing up in Washington, DC, and now living in Michigan, meant I automatically associated Christmas with cold and snow. As contrary as it seemed since I'd been the one to insist on a warm honeymoon, I was secretly glad we'd be back home a few days before Christmas. The cruise line tried, but Christmas here wouldn't have cut it.

Of the three other couples we shared our table with, only one pair was there as I took my seat.

The dining room wasn't the only place to eat on the ship, but so far everyone had attended all the meals. Since we were having our first at-sea day, I knew none of them were off ship.

I swiveled in my seat. Except for our table, the dining room looked as full as usual.

Maybe Mark's food poisoning guess wasn't as far off as it originally sounded. We would have all been served at the same time. If the others had whatever Mark had last night, they might be sick, too. If I remembered correctly, I'd had the chicken, while most of the others had fish. I'd never been a fan of salmon, and no one made fish as delicious as A Salt and Battery back home.

I could almost hear my mother's voice in my head. *Don't go looking for trouble, Nicole. Enough will find you on its own.*

My subconscious mom-voice might be right. I'd been going a little stir-crazy spending all day in our room. Mark had either been throwing up or sleeping, so I'd stayed in the room with him to keep an eye on him rather than partaking of any of the ship's amenities. I'd finished the book I'd been reading a few hours ago, and I was tired of playing Sudoku on my phone. My brain might be looking for another puzzle to solve.

But if many members of our table had gotten food poisoning, didn't I have a responsibility to report it? Surely the kitchen would want to investigate so that it wouldn't happen again.

Besides, if Mark had food poisoning, I could stop worrying that he'd contracted some sort of plague before we even set foot on South American soil.

It wouldn't hurt for me to stop by the cabin of the couple who usually sat next to me. They were on their honeymoon as well, but the wife, Carrie, had said she was more interested in excursions than her husband was. That wasn't surprising in itself. They looked like they were close to twenty years different in age, and her husband was heavyset. Carrie had given me their cabin number in case we came across something I wanted to do that Mark didn't. She'd said she'd be game for anything.

I almost left before dessert until I saw they were serving a maple syrup mousse. Then my curiosity wouldn't let me leave. If it was good, I'd try to weasel a recipe out of the chef before we left the ship. These days, I was always on the lookout for more maple syrup recipes. Living on a maple syrup farm tended to have that effect.

The mousse was silky and maple-ly and everything I'd been hoping for. It also stuck in my throat. It didn't seem fair for Mark to have to miss out.

I left my goblet without finishing it. The sooner I figured out whether or not he had food poisoning, the better. If it was food poisoning, it'd pass on its own within a day or two, and we could look forward to enjoying the rest of the trip together.

Carrie and her husband didn't have an ocean-view cabin, either, based on the cabin number she'd given me. Mark and I had wanted one, but they'd all been booked by the time we reserved our tickets—one of the drawbacks of having a short engagement. It was something else Carrie and I had bonded over. She and Garth had married even quicker than Mark and I had. They'd only known each other six weeks.

I was glad to leave "Jingle Bells" behind and exit into the relative quiet of the corridors. Mark being sick must be making me extra grumpy because I normally loved Christmas carols.

I was thankful the corridors weren't completely empty, though. I had to stop three separate people for directions. It was too bad they didn't make GPS maps of cruise ships. Not being able to find my way around on my own was getting a little embarrassing.

At least I'd had my exercise for the day by the time I reached their cabin.

I knocked on the door. A small sound came from inside, but I couldn't be sure what it was or if I'd even really heard anything. Cruise ships had a whole set of noises to themselves. There was the almost imperceptible drone of the engines and the water rushing by, but there was also the faint groaning sound as the water pressed against the hull and the murmur that seemed to accompany any situation where hundreds of people packed into a space together.

A family passed me, and the little girl stared at me on her way by. Heat crept up my neck. Maybe this was a silly idea after all. For all I knew, they'd been too busy doing other things and had lost track of time. They were on their honeymoon, after all.

The memory of Mark leaning over a trash can filled my mind. I'd knock one more time, awkwardness notwithstanding. If I could get to the bottom of why he was sick, I should, especially if it would prevent it happening to someone else in the future. Besides, if they were both sick, they might want me to bring them something.

I knocked louder this time. "Carrie, it's Nicole. From your dinner table. You said I should stop by."

That was only a minor warping of the truth, right? I wasn't exactly here to invite her to anything.

This time I was sure I heard someone moving inside.

The door slid open a crack, the safety chain still in place.

Carrie's face peeked out. "I'm not feeling up to doing anything, but thanks for checking."

Her answer made it sound like she wasn't feeling well. Her hair was the beautiful sun-kissed blonde that no one was actually born with. Prior to today, she'd always had it carefully curled. Now she wore it straight and back in a ponytail. It was what I imagined she'd do if she planned to stay in all day rather than coming out. If she wasn't feeling well, she wouldn't have bothered styling her hair.

But then why the safety chain?

I wanted to give myself a swift kick in the shins. I needed to learn how to shut my lawyer's brain off or I was never going to be able to relax enough to enjoy this trip once Mark recovered. She'd probably put the chain on before she knew it was me.

Though, she could have looked out the peephole. And I had told her who was outside the door.

"I'll see you another day," Carrie said while sliding the door shut.

"Wait." I held up a hand but didn't put it into the door in case she continued to close it. I wasn't about to lose any fingers over what could still be a wild goose chase. "Are you feeling okay? I think Mark might have gotten food poisoning, and I was checking to see if anyone else from our table was feeling sick after last night's meal."

The door wobbled like Carrie couldn't decide whether to open it farther or continue to close it.

She didn't look sick the way Mark did, but she didn't look entirely well, either. Dark circles showed through her makeup, and I could have sworn that her eyes were red like she'd either been crying or struggling not to.

She swallowed hard enough that I could see it bob in her throat. "What kind of lawyer did you say you were again?"

A tingle ran up my arms, like all the hairs wanted to stand at attention. "Criminal defense attorney." I didn't want to ask, but I couldn't help myself. "Why?"

Carrie slid the safety chain off her door. "I think I might need one."

CHAPTER 2

The words *I think I need a lawyer* ranked very close to the top of the list of things I *didn't* want to hear on my honeymoon. In fact, the only thing I could think of that would be above it was *I'm sorry, brand-new Mrs. Cavanaugh, but your husband has the bubonic plague, and he's going to die.*

Carrie had whispered the words, and now her eyes were growing larger, like she had a fear of spiders and one was crawling ever closer to her.

Great. Just great. It wasn't like I could walk away and leave her in her room, freaking out. Especially if she had her husband's dead body in there.

If she did, he'd probably died of natural causes. She was probably panicking and didn't know what to do. My only hope was that he'd died with his clothes on rather than in the shower or in some other embarrassing situation. I did not want to go in if that was the case.

But if she had killed someone… "Before you tell me anything, I need to let you know that I only defend clients who are innocent."

I would have sworn she looked excited at that announcement.

"Like Matlock? My dad and I used to watch *Matlock* together all the time. I need a Matlock."

This woman didn't strike me as a killer, but I could say that about a lot of murderers I'd met in the past year. The smartest ones were often the ones who knew how to deflect suspicion.

I also didn't know if her answer meant she was innocent or guilty.

If she really had killed her husband—or someone else—I'd stay long enough to convince her to call security and then refer her to someone who represented guilty clients…and *wasn't* on their honeymoon. If she had the money to pay their fees, my parents were the best in the business at setting guilty people free.

When I told my children one day what their grandparents did for a living, I probably didn't want to phrase it that way.

What kind of a mom would I be if I couldn't even manage to stay with my husband on our honeymoon? The sooner I got this managed, the sooner I could buy Mark's ginger ale and head back to our cabin. "Why don't you tell me what happened?"

She slid the safety chain off the door and opened it wide

enough for me to slide in sideways, like she was afraid someone would haul her away based on the mere sight of whatever was inside.

For the rest of this trip, if someone asked me what I did for a living, I was going to tell them I was a preschool teacher.

Carrie shut the door behind me and put the chain back in place.

Their cabin looked like it was hit by a tropical storm. Everything from the top of the desk had been swiped onto the floor, and the chair lay on its side. The bedding lay scattered across the room.

It looked more like the room of someone who'd been robbed than someone who'd been murdered.

What I didn't see was a body. Or any blood.

Carrie had a fragile look to her, like someone who exercised too much and didn't eat enough. Her chin formed a sharp triangle point in her narrow face. She definitely didn't look strong enough to haul a body down the hallway and toss it into the ocean—assuming she could have done that without being spotted.

I turned back to face her. "I'm confused. Why do you think you need a lawyer?"

"This is what the room looked like when I came back from my workout this morning. Garth wasn't here, and he isn't answering my texts or anything."

She moved toward the bed like she needed to sit, but

stopped again before touching it. She seemed to have a sense that if this were a crime scene, she shouldn't compromise the evidence.

How long had she been standing, afraid to touch anything by sitting? Had she been sitting on the toilet lid or the side of the tub all day?

Not reporting the tossed room right away would be hard for her to explain, but it didn't mean she needed a lawyer. From the look of it, she had reason to be concerned for her husband, but not reason to be concerned that someone would want to blame her for whatever had happened to him. "We need to contact security."

She shook her head and backed a step away from me. "They'll blame me."

Clearly we needed to rewind a few steps. Maybe she didn't understand how the law worked. I'd seen it a few times before back in DC when we encountered a client whose family immigrated from another country where laws and customs were different. *Due process* and *innocent until proven guilty* weren't universal standards.

In the United States, she couldn't be held responsible for her husband's death if she hadn't been involved. More importantly, we didn't even know anything had happened to her husband yet. "Someone broke into your room while you weren't here. There's nothing you could do about that."

She sank down onto the floor and sat cross-legged. That

answered my question about where she'd been sitting for the past eight or so hours.

"His family thought from the start that I was marrying him for his money." Her voice had an edge to it—a little bit scared and a little bit angry. "They didn't think I could love someone so much older so fast. I signed a prenup, but Jeremy—his son—said prenups only mattered if he divorced me, not if I killed him. He said if anything happened to his dad, he'd know it was me, and he'd make sure the police knew."

Garth's son sounded like a gem, as my grandma would have said. That said, I likely would have felt the same way and suspected the same things if my mom was gone and my dad married a much younger woman.

Carrie's voice was ramping up in volume and pitch.

We didn't need anyone passing by to hear her. Cruise ships probably didn't have the same rumor mill as Fair Haven did, but that didn't mean word wouldn't still get around about a hysterical woman yelling about killing someone.

I patted the air in a shushing motion.

She gulped in a breath. "It doesn't matter what really happened. If anything bad happens to Garth, Jeremy will think I was involved." She'd brought her voice back down to a normal level, but now she dropped it even lower. "I left the door propped open with a pen. Garth said it was okay because he wasn't going anywhere, and I didn't want to take my key card."

She patted her tight shorts as if to say *no pockets*. Now that I had a closer look at her, she did still seem to be in workout clothes. She hadn't showered or changed.

Leaving the door propped open didn't look good. Any worthwhile prosecutor would argue she'd done it to give easy access to their room to whoever she hired to kill or kidnap her husband. They'd say she made it up that Garth agreed to it. They'd say a lot of things given the age difference and the prenuptial agreement.

Still, we couldn't sit here doing nothing. "You know we have to report this. Otherwise you wouldn't have asked me in here."

She nodded her head.

I waited, but she didn't levy any more arguments at me. If she knew that, then what she wanted before we called security was reassurance that she wouldn't have to face the questions alone.

She wanted some line of defense in case someone wanted to implicate her. I couldn't blame her. The spouse or significant other was always the first person the police looked at. Many people often had a fear—not entirely unfounded—that if they said something wrong or acted in a way the police viewed as suspicious, attention would turn to them even if they weren't guilty.

Having a lawyer by your side from the start could make you look guilty. It could also help protect you if you weren't.

I held out a hand to lift her to her feet. "Do you want to call or should I?"

CHAPTER 3

Carrie held the shipboard phone in one hand, her other hovering over the buttons. "Do I tell them I think something bad happened to Garth?"

The way her bottom lip quivered told me she shouldn't make the call at all. She'd be likely to fill the security officer's ear with all her fears about what happened to Garth and how her son-in-law would want to blame her.

Right now, we didn't actually know what had happened. In fact, we didn't know that Garth hadn't fallen asleep out on the deck with his ringer turned off on his cell phone. Or maybe, judging by the state of the room, he'd had an argument on the phone and was walking around, trying to calm down before returning to his cabin. A nasty business call could ruin someone's mood on their honeymoon, and maybe he simply hadn't wanted to take it out on his new wife.

There were still a lot of scenarios that didn't add up to fingers pointed at Carrie.

I stretched out my hand, palm up. "Maybe it'd be better if I did it."

She tossed the receiver to me like it burned her. I missed the catch, and the cord yanked it back, setting it swinging. I scooped it up.

Instead of throwing a bunch of details at the security officer, I told him my friend came back from working out and found her room had been disrupted. She hasn't been able to reach her husband, and she's scared.

In the time it took someone to reach us, I prepped Carrie to only answer what she was asked and to not mention her fears about being blamed.

The man who knocked on the door less than ten minutes later looked awfully young, with a haircut that said he'd gotten this job straight out of the military and was more used to breaking up drunken arguments than investigating crimes.

The way he ogled Carrie also told me he would have flirted with her had she not been wearing a wedding ring—and a big, flashy one at that.

His obvious attraction seemed to play in our favor, at least. He didn't seem to suspect she'd had anything to do with what happened, and he offered to carry her bags to another room. The current room, he said, would have to be locked down until his manager decided what to do.

He also promised to personally help search the ship for her husband.

He lifted her bag like it was nothing and held the door open for us to leave.

"I have to go take care of Mark," I whispered to Carrie. "I'll check in on you later, okay?"

She nodded and trailed after the security officer like she wouldn't have known what to do if someone wasn't leading the way.

Anyone would have assumed she'd married Garth for money, especially given the size of her diamond. But I had a feeling it was more that she'd been looking for a sense of stability and someone to do the thinking for her. She wanted to be taken care of, and a well-off man so much her elder would have been a perfect fit.

The ship intercom system started paging Garth Bodie as I was paying for a bottle of ginger ale for Mark.

I'd been gone a lot longer than I'd expected to be when I'd left the room for dinner. Any minute now, Mark would probably start to worry about me. The last thing I wanted to do was worry my sick husband.

Besides, I shouldn't have left him alone this long when he was sick.

Maybe I wasn't going to be very good at this wife thing. I'd hoped it would come naturally. I'd get married and just magically know how to live as a married woman and how to balance my relationship with my work. I should have known better. My parents weren't your normal couple. They both worked long hours, and conversation around our dinner table had been mostly case-related. A proper work–life balance—or even how to take a vacation—wasn't in my DNA.

I added a package of saltine crackers to my purchase and headed back to our cabin. I only made one wrong turn this time. Navigating the cruise ship made me miss Fair Haven. I could get almost everywhere I needed to by now without a GPS.

Mark was sitting up in bed when I entered. I tore open the crackers, poured him a glass of ginger ale, and climbed up onto the bed next to him.

What was the right thing to do here? Did I tell him what happened with Carrie, or did I let him rest?

It was one of those relationship moments that I just didn't know how to handle. If I told him, it could seem inconsiderate. He was sick and needed to rest. He didn't need me running around and dealing with someone else's problems rather than caring for him.

On the other hand, if I didn't tell him and he found out later, he might feel like I was keeping things from him. I'd set a rule early on that I wouldn't keep secrets from Mark. That was one of the positive lessons I'd taken away from my parents' marriage. They might lie to everyone else, including me, but they didn't lie to each other.

I also knew that secrets among members in the Cavanaugh

family were a crime up there with stealing. I was a Cavanaugh now, albeit by marriage.

But I couldn't quite bring myself to tell him I'd fallen into the middle of a mystery on our honeymoon. "Do you want to hear about an interesting puzzle?"

Mark quirked an eyebrow at me, a sign the ginger ale and crackers were making him feel a little better. "If you were anyone else, I'd think you meant a riddle. Please tell me that at least there's no dead body involved."

One of the things I loved so much about Mark was that he understood me in a way that no one else seemed to. Unfortunately, that tended to also backfire on me at times. "No dead body." I mouthed the words *at present*.

Mark must have read my lips because he rested his head back against the headboard. "I'll take what I can get. Whatever your puzzle is will be better than thinking about my rolling stomach."

He was a doctor. Even though as the county medical examiner he usually worked with dead people, he'd gone to medical school. He should know whether what he had was food poisoning or something more serious. I had to trust that this would pass within a couple of days.

In a weird way, I was glad it wasn't me. If I were the sick one, people would assume I was already pregnant.

In the meantime, I could distract Mark. That was something I could do to help.

I explained to Mark why I'd gone to Carrie's room and what I found there.

"That's only marginally better than a dead body being involved," he said when I finished. "At least it's not a murder."

I popped one of the crackers into my mouth. I wasn't really hungry, but I was a stress eater, and the crackers were all I had handy. "I'm afraid it might be. Or a kidnapping."

Mark took a slow sip of his ginger ale. "It could be, but the mess in the room sounds like it also could have happened from something less suspicious."

While I had more experience dealing with criminals one-on-one, Mark had seen more crime scenes than I ever would, even if I worked until I was eighty.

He handed me his empty glass. "Garth Bodie is an over-weight man in his late fifties, early sixties. It sounds like he might have felt dizzy when he got out of bed, lost his balance, and tipped over the chair and wiped everything off the desk in a fall."

I understood what Mark wasn't saying. He didn't think Garth had been murdered and tossed overboard or kidnapped for ransom. He thought Garth felt sick, left his room to head for the shipboard infirmary, and collapsed with either a heart attack or stroke.

"Wouldn't someone have spotted him if he went for help and didn't make it?"

"Not if he collapsed in a stairwell. Most people take the elevators. Even the staff."

Crap. He was right. If Garth had been trying to reach the infirmary quickly and wasn't thinking straight, he might have opted for the stairs rather than waiting for the elevator.

"I'm going to try to fall asleep while you go check," Mark said.

I leaned over and kissed him, plague possibility notwithstanding. He knew I wouldn't be able to rest or think about anything else if Garth Bodie might be lying somewhere, still alive and in need of medical attention.

CHAPTER 4

I spent the next hour checking every possible route from Carrie and Garth's cabin to the shipboard infirmary. As far as I could tell, Garth wasn't in any of the stairwells, or anywhere else, for that matter. Given how many times I got turned around, I was certain he hadn't collapsed anywhere along a false path, either.

It wasn't until I finished that I realized I'd been wandering around in stairwells alone on a ship that might have a murderer also running loose. It showed either how sick Mark was or how convinced he was that Garth disappeared of natural causes that he hadn't thought of it, either.

I turned to head back to our cabin but stopped. I hadn't heard them page Garth over the intercom system recently. It had to have been at least twenty minutes. They'd been calling for Garth

Bodie to report to one of the concierge desks every ten minutes
prior to now.

That could mean only one of two things. Either they'd found
him or they'd decided he wasn't going to respond. My watch
showed me that it'd been close to two hours since the first page.

The timeline matched with them giving up on him answering. If he hadn't showed up within ninety minutes, he wasn't
likely to respond.

I needed to check in with Carrie and find out what was
happening before I reported back to Mark. Hopefully he'd been
able to fall asleep. One of us should get some rest. My mind
certainly wasn't going to shut down enough for a decent sleep
until someone found Garth Bodie.

I'd thought Carrie's new room number was 713, but when I
knocked on the door, a thirteen-year-old boy answered. He gave
me a look that said he wanted to tell his parents that some weird
lady was at the door. Definitely not Carrie's room.

I knocked on 731 instead. "Carrie?"

The door flew open—a vastly different reception than I'd
gotten last time—and a woman threw herself into my arms.

It had to be Carrie, but it happened so fast that I didn't get a
look at her face. My parents would lecture me about professional
distance. I didn't care. This wasn't about making money. I didn't
even want to be acting as a lawyer right now. I was in this as a
friend. Carrie seemed like she needed one of those more than she
needed a lawyer.

She pulled me into the room and shut the door behind her.

She'd showered and changed into shorts and a top that revealed her midriff. She wasn't wearing any makeup. Without it, she looked younger even than I'd guessed before. Younger than I was.

As much as I hated to admit it, I could see why Garth's son might be suspicious. Jeremy was probably at least ten years older than his new stepmother.

Her reaction to seeing me told me what I'd suspected—Garth hadn't turned up yet. "Do you have any news?" I asked.

She dropped down onto the bed with enough force that she bounced. "Nothing. They've searched the ship and paged him for an hour." The look on her face reminded me of someone who'd just discovered that all the money had been drained from their bank accounts. "Do you think he fell overboard?"

Possible but not probable, as Mark liked to say. If Garth had a health scare and had gone for help, he didn't need to go above-board to reach the infirmary. Even if he'd gotten turned around, he wouldn't likely have gotten outside and fallen over. It was even less likely he'd have done so without being noticed.

I sank down onto the bed beside her. "I doubt it."

With everyone, including me, searching for him, it also seemed less and less likely that he'd collapsed on his way to the infirmary.

Carrie grabbed my hand and held onto it like she was the one afraid of falling overboard and drowning. "You said you were like Matlock. Will you help me figure out what happened to him?"

I hadn't actually said I was like Matlock. I'd said I defended innocent people, and she'd filled in the Matlock part.

Setting that aside, there was a more important hurdle. "I'm on my honeymoon."

Carrie wrapped her other hand around mine. I couldn't have gone anywhere even if I'd tried. Not without knocking her over.

"Please," she said. "I have no one else to turn to."

She didn't have to say *It's my honeymoon, too*. In fact, she probably hadn't even meant to imply it.

I heard it anyway. It was like I'd unintentionally flown into a planet's gravitational pull, and I couldn't break free.

I knew now that my compassion for people was one of my strengths, not a weakness the way my dad always seemed to think. In this case, though, I wasn't sure what the right thing to do was. It didn't seem right to leave my new husband sick in our cabin to chase after a missing person. It also didn't seem right to leave Carrie to sit alone in her cabin, afraid and uncertain about what happened to her husband.

Mark had said *for better or for worse*, the same way I'd said *in sickness and in health*. I knew he'd forgive me if I did this. Maybe it proved that I wasn't going to be a good wife, because I was counting on that forgiveness, but if I didn't help Carrie, I wasn't sure I could forgive myself.

I squeezed her hand. "I'll try."

It took the next five minutes to get Carrie to stop hugging me. It reminded me again of how young she was. Too young to have to deal with something like this on her honeymoon. When she'd married a significantly older man, she'd hopefully done so knowing she'd be widowed young. I suspected, though, that she hadn't figured on being widowed *this* young.

With Garth not responding to pages or showing up in the search, that might well be what she'd face.

Carrie would figure out soon enough that her husband was no longer alive. I wasn't going to be the one to tell her, especially since there was a small chance I was wrong. We could hope for the best and plan for the worst, as my grandma used to tell me to do.

I suddenly missed my grandma. She seemed like she would have had good advice for me on how to be a wife and working woman. She'd worked as a nurse alongside my grandpa in his practice.

Now wasn't the time to think about my own problems, though. Carrie's were much more serious and pressing.

What we were hunting for now was justice and closure. Carrie didn't need to live for the rest of her life with people wondering if she'd been the one to kill her husband, if he was dead. And whoever had harmed or taken Garth should be brought to justice.

We didn't have long to achieve both those goals. Once this cruise was over, everyone would go their separate ways, making it nearly impossible to question anyone. The perpetrator could slip through the cracks. That might even be why they'd planned their crime for this moment. Given the small window of time and how well they'd hidden Garth away, it seemed safe to assume it had been premeditated.

Their room looked at first glance like it'd been a robbery. Most thefts on a cruise ship were crimes of opportunity—someone left their jewelry lying around and the cleaning crew couldn't withstand the temptation, or someone forgot their cell phone on the deck and it wasn't there when they went back. Breaking into a room and tossing it didn't fit with either of those.

We should look and see if anything was missing. If something was, it could help us prove who did it. It'd also be good info to give to ship's security for when they had enough evidence to question a suspect.

They might even be able to search a room for it. I honestly didn't know what the law was about searching a person of interest's room on a cruise ship out at sea. Police weren't allowed to search a rented hotel room without a warrant any more than they were allowed to search a private residence without a warrant. But that was in American territory and not on a cruise ship in international waters. Things might be different here.

Either way, that was a moot point until we knew if anything

was missing. If nothing was, then we'd know this had been personal and not about stealing something at all. If nothing was missing, then the mess was either due to a struggle or whoever took Garth wanted it to look like the room was robbed.

I called the security office and told them we needed to get back into Carrie's original cabin because she'd forgotten a few things. I put the handset back into the cradle and turned around.

Carrie was staring at me. "You lied to them."

The way she said it made me think I might have put a crack in her image of me as a female Matlock. "They wouldn't have let us back into your room otherwise."

"It's not that." She gave a cringe-shiver. "If I hadn't known you were lying, I wouldn't have been able to tell. My ex-boyfriend used to take advantage of that all the time. I was hoping I'd get better at knowing, but it looks like I'm not."

I wasn't sure whether I felt sorry for her or envied her. That level of innocence could put her in danger of being used, but it would also be so freeing to not instinctively question everyone and their motives. My brain picked up too many small details and tells for me to ever have the kind of rest and confidence that Carrie would have.

But if I had peace, I also wouldn't have a career. It was a trade I was willing to make to feel like I was doing something good and worthwhile.

Carrie walked beside me down the corridor. I had to take two strides for every one she took. It wasn't just the length of her strides that struck me, either. She had a natural grace, like a ballerina.

She slowed, making it easier for me to keep up. "What are we looking for?"

"Anything that should be there and isn't."

In some ways, looking for what was missing here was easier than if we'd needed to look for something out of place or missing in a home. Most people knew what they'd packed for a trip and could make a mental list. She might have a more difficult time knowing which of Garth's possessions were missing, unfortunately. She wouldn't have packed his bags.

Carrie gave a sharp nod and put on what I imagined was her game face. Her expression had a strange scrunchiness to it, like she was concentrating hard.

The same security officer who'd responded to our earlier call waited for us outside their original cabin door. He unlocked the door with a swipe of his key card. "I can't let you go in alone. My boss is waiting for instructions from corporate on what to do with the room."

Carrie might not realize what that meant, but I did. They didn't believe Garth Bodie was on the ship anymore. They might not think any foul play had happened, but they did know they had a missing passenger who'd either disembarked without being properly logged out at our last American stop or who'd gone overboard at some point along the way. Or was dead and stuffed into the bowels of the ship somewhere where no one would find him without knowing where to look.

I wouldn't be much help in knowing what was missing and what wasn't, but I didn't want the security officer to question why I was here if it wasn't to help. "I'll collect up those items we talked about from the bathroom," I said.

For a second Carrie looked confused. She really wasn't good at play acting. Then she nodded. "Thank you." Her words squeaked out.

The security officer must have thought she was simply upset. He solicitously held the door open. "You first, ma'am."

Carrie headed for the main part of the cabin, and I ducked into the bathroom. There were two sets of toiletries resting on the edge of the tub. Carrie must have actually forgotten to grab her shampoo and conditioner when she packed up her belongings earlier. I scooped up the ones that looked like they were feminine.

I turned in a circle and pulled open the drawers, but there was nothing more in the bathroom. Carrie really must have been struggling to think clearly if she took Garth's toothbrush and deodorant and forgot her own shampoo.

"Our passports," Carrie said from the other room, her voice unnaturally loud as if she wanted me to hear. "That's one of the things I forgot. And Garth's wallet. I wouldn't have been able to sleep if I left them here."

That last part had to be for the benefit of the security officer.

I exited the bathroom, her shampoo and conditioner in my hands. "I got the rest."

"That's everything then," Carrie said.

The security officer practically tripped over his own feet trying to get to the door to open it for her. I didn't blame him. I thought Carrie was more beautiful without all the heavy makeup she usually wore, too.

"Do you need me to see you back to your room?" he asked.

Carrie opened her mouth, closed it, then looked at me.

"I'm going with her, but thank you."

He gave her one more smile, tugged on the door of the room, and left.

I waited until he was out of earshot. "Was anything missing?"

She held open Garth's wallet. At least two hundred dollars nestled inside. "Nothing. Not even his cash."

They left Carrie and Garth's passports behind, too. They weren't looking to steal and sell identities.

That meant this was most likely personal. Whoever broke into their room did so to get at Garth. The room was either disrupted in the ensuing struggle or the perpetrator did it to make it look like a robbery.

There hadn't been any blood, though. Garth had probably been alive when he left the room. I suspected they threatened that they'd hurt Carrie unless he came quietly. There weren't many other reasons a man would go with someone who likely wanted to hurt him. Threatening a loved one had been how my Uncle Stan's murderer convinced him to do things he hadn't wanted to do.

Unfortunately, just because he left alive didn't mean he was still alive. They might have taken him for a ransom, or they might have simply wanted to kill him someplace more private, where it would be easier to dispose of his body without being spotted.

Carrie watched me as if she were trying—and failing—to figure out what I was thinking. "What do we do next? If this wasn't robbery?"

The way she said it made me think she suspected that it wasn't robbery, but she still needed my reassurance.

"It doesn't look like robbery. So now we need to figure out who might have wanted to hurt Garth."

CHAPTER 5

"There are hundreds of people on this ship," I said. "We have to try to narrow it down. Was there anyone on board who knew Garth?"

Carrie fiddled with one of her dangly earrings. "I'm not sure. I haven't known him long enough to know all the people he might know. He didn't say he saw anyone he knew, though, if that helps."

Not really.

Their short romance could make this case close to impossible. Then again, I'd once defended a man whose whole defense was that he'd hallucinated a grizzly bear. I felt like making the joke that my middle name was Impossible Cases, but the thought of adding that mouthful to my already ungainly name made me want to cringe.

Besides, no one, not even Matlock—heck, not even my parents—succeeded in all their cases. I didn't want to give Carrie false hope. This time, I might fail.

But I'd do my best to make sure that didn't happen.

"What about anyone who acted strangely around him? Or did he have an argument with anyone?"

Carrie shook her head, then stopped and tugged on her earring. Her earlobe extended far enough that it looked like she was going to rip through it. "Garth told me about one guy he thought was going to hit him. The guy didn't, though."

She said it like the fact that he didn't hit Garth and only wanted to made him not a viable suspect. "You weren't there?"

She let go of her ear. "Garth didn't want me going to his poker games." She smiled in a way that filled her whole face. "He said it was no place for a lady. No one ever called me a lady before."

Part of me wondered where Carrie and Garth had met. I reined my curiosity in. Unless it was pertinent to the case, it was none of my business, and I'd been accused of being too curious for my own good. Carrie would tell me eventually if she wanted to. If I had to guess, however, I might guess someplace with exotic dancers.

Since she hadn't seen the argument, she wouldn't be able to describe the man, but that shouldn't matter. "The ship's casino probably has cameras. Most casinos do, to stop cheating. We'll be able to ask security to check their recordings."

Carrie was shaking her head hard enough it set her earrings bobbing before I even finished. "It wasn't a public game. Garth didn't like the limits and rules the ship set."

Well, that definitely gave us a place to start—*and* added a problem. "If the game wasn't legal, we'll have a hard time finding out who was there. And then getting anyone to admit to being there and seeing anything even if we do."

Carrie mushed up her lips. "The game was legal. Garth told me. They waited until we were in international waters, he said. He had to be right, because it was a staff member who told him about the game."

I didn't know whether to massage the band of tension that bloomed above my eyebrows or be excited by the lead. The game might be legal in international waters, but staff probably had it in their contract that they couldn't engage in outside gambling.

"Did Garth tell you the man's name?"

"Nope. But I know who he is. He works in the fitness center. I took a class with him yesterday."

If he worked in the fitness center, he might have also known that Carrie routinely worked out at the same time every day. It was too soon to say, but I felt like stealing a phrase from one of my favorite TV detectives—Monk. He might be the guy.

I turned Carrie around and headed us in the direction I

thought would bring us to the security office. Carrie had to redirect us once. I counted that as improvement.

The man sitting behind the desk in the security office glanced up as we entered. His gaze landed on the bottles of shampoo and conditioner in my hands. Maybe we should have dropped them by Carrie's cabin prior to coming, but the longer we waited, the lesser our chances that Garth might still be alive. And the lesser our chances that we'd catch his killer if he wasn't.

I shifted the bottles to put them behind my back, but that made my chest stick out, like I wanted him to look at it. Which he then did.

Heat rose up my neck, scorching my skin enough to set my t-shirt on fire. I brought the bottles back to the front and tucked them into the nook of one arm. "We need to speak to whoever is in charge of the search for Garth Bodie."

He gave me a look that would have been a sigh if it were audible. "That's me."

"I'm his wife," Carrie blurted.

At least she picked up on the fact that the man was going to have a hard time taking us seriously. It might have been better to take the extra few minutes so we didn't show up with arms full of toiletries.

I moved forward one step. "Carrie remembered someone who had a disagreement with Garth. We thought it was possible he might have had something to do with Garth's disappearance."

The man did sigh this time. It reminded me a bit of Chief McTavish every time I brought some crazy idea into his office. "I know you're worried about him, but life isn't like TV shows." He smiled, but his lips looked made from plastic. "I promise you that this is probably all a misunderstanding. Even if it isn't, I guarantee that nothing criminal happened here."

I squinted at his name tag. Hart. The rest of the staff on the cruise ship had first names on their name tags. It figured the security officers wouldn't. It automatically gave them more authority. When you only knew a person's last name, you tended to add *Ms.* or *Mr.* in front. It was a psychological trick. A smart one. Carrie already looked like she was ready to give up and back away.

I handed her the shampoo and conditioner and pulled out my phone. Hopefully he'd think I planned to use it to take notes.

I knew how my mom would handle this situation. Given what a delay could mean, I was going to have to borrow her tactics. They worked, even if they weren't always the way I wanted to deal with people.

I put on a smile that I hoped was a good imitation of my mom's—her smile had just enough warmth to bring down people's defenses and enough cold steel to say *Don't mess with me*. I held out a hand. "I forgot to introduce myself. Nicole Fitzhenry-Dawes of Taylor Fitzhenry-Dawes, LLC. I'm the Bodies' attorney."

"Their attorney." His tone said *What kind of people bring their attorney with them on vacation?* like he suddenly thought the whole thing might be a set-up.

"And friend," I added. "Right now, we don't know for sure what the situation is with Mr. Bodie. Mrs. Bodie"—I swept my hand toward Carrie, who looked a bit like a spooked deer—"and I think it would be best to treat this as a worst-case scenario rather than not taking it seriously enough and opening the cruise line up to a lawsuit down the road."

Lawsuits weren't the kind of law I practiced, but Hart didn't need to know that.

The look he gave me was that mingling of fear, anger, and frustration that people got when you pressed their hand. It made me feel like one of those slime ball ambulance-chasing lawyers on TV.

Please let him give in, I prayed.

I didn't want to have to push things further and suggest I could escalate this to whoever was above him. I wasn't against doing that if I had to. A life was at stake. I just didn't want to make this man feel smaller than I already had. My mom might have had no problem doing so, but it wasn't the way I would want to be treated, so I didn't want to treat anyone else that way, either.

He got up from his desk. "You have to understand that I've never investigated a missing person's case before. What next step do you and Mrs. Bodie feel would be appropriate?"

Bingo. My mom would be so proud. The man clearly valued his job over his pride, which made sense. Unfortunately, many people in the service industries had to. They weren't always treated well by patrons.

I also got the impression that he didn't think this was anything serious, but he was willing to humor us rather than have us stir up trouble with the main office.

If humoring us meant he let me take point on this, then I'd go with it. He could think he was humoring me all he wanted. I opened my mouth to tell him we wanted him to question a person of interest as to his whereabouts during the window of opportunity.

I stopped before the first word came out. If I phrased it that way, he really would think I'd been watching too much TV, and then he'd ignore me, lawyer or not. "Mr. Bodie had a confrontation with a staff member during an unsanctioned poker game. We think there could have been continuing animosity that got out of hand."

That sounded professional and not TV-ish.

For a second, an *oh crap* look flashed across his face. He might have liked it better if we'd named a passenger. If we were wrong, he'd have to face a hostile staff member every trip in perpetuity. Assuming this didn't get the man fired.

Hart straightened up and pulled his shoulders back. "And what is this man's name?"

"It's either Nat or Nick." Carrie hugged the shampoo and

conditioner to her body. "I don't remember exactly, but he works in the fitness center."

"It's Nat," Hart said.

His voice was deadpan. I couldn't read anything from it. Which left me unsure as to whether to be impressed that he knew every staff member by name or to read into it that this particular man had caused him trouble in the past.

"I'll deal with the poker game separately." He picked up the receiver of the phone on his desk. "Let me give him a call about where he was this morning. We might be able to resolve this quickly."

That was smart, actually. It wouldn't tip our hand. Assuming Nat had been involved, if he showed up here and saw Carrie, he'd be instantly on his guard. To avoid that, we would have needed to leave. I'd rather stay and be able to hear what was going on. Hart hadn't dealt with criminals and criminal cases before. I had.

You put yourself in a position of authority, my mom's advice played in my head as if she were standing next to me. *Now make him feel like your equal again so that you'll have an ally.*

I held up my pointer finger in a one-second gesture. "Could you put him on speaker, please?" I leaned forward as if I was about to share a secret and inclined my head toward Carrie. "That way we can set Mrs. Bodie's mind at ease."

I was hoping he'd hear *I want to resolve this quickly, too.*

His hand hovered over the buttons for a full two breaths. By the third, I held mine.

Finally, he set the receiver on his desk. "Of course."

Now I'd hope that I was right that Hart would come at this sideways in order to avoid a co-worker out for revenge.

He dialed. A woman picked up, and he asked if Nat was available. The line switched over to canned music. I guess even on cruise ships they wanted people to know that they hadn't been disconnected, and the only way they could think of to do that was to play music no one would want to listen to normally.

The music stopped.

"This is Nat," a man's voice said.

"It's Rick Hart. I had a couple of things I needed to clear up with you just so I can get the paperwork off my desk."

My respect for Hart inched up. I still had a suspicion that his approach was about keeping his own neck off the target block if Nat wasn't involved in this, but he knew how to come at things without raising people's suspicions. It was probably a skill he'd developed working the cruise ship. He'd have needed to approach anything with a passenger carefully. The last thing he'd have wanted was rumors or fear-mongering onboard.

"Were you working this morning?" Hart asked.

"Yeah." Nat's voice took on a cautious edge. "Yoga from six to seven, and then spin class from seven-thirty until eight. Then I had a private training session. Why?"

Those time frames put him in the fitness center at the same

time as Carrie. Conceivably he might have been able to run to their room and beat Carrie there, but it wouldn't have left any time for a confrontation with Garth.

Hart tapped his fingers against his leg. "Nothing to worry about. I had a complaint that the classes were too full, is all, and that it posed a hazard. Did you have many people?"

Nat gave numbers that I assumed were well within capacity. "I can bring you the sign-in sheets on my next break."

"If you wouldn't mind."

Also smart. Any or all of those people could confirm Nat's whereabouts during the time.

Leaving us with the problem of having eliminated our only viable suspect at the moment. Maybe someone else from the game had wanted to hurt Garth. They could have seen the argument between the two and thought they had an opportunity to get rid of Garth while creating reasonable doubt since Nat would seem like he had a motive.

I waved a hand. Hart looked my way.

"Ask about the argument," I mouthed.

Hart frowned. For a second, I couldn't tell whether he didn't want to ask or didn't understand.

He inclined his head forward slightly and lifted his hands.

He didn't know what I was trying to say.

I mimed dealing cards.

Hart shrugged.

"You still there?" Nat asked.

"Just…uh…" Hart glanced at his desk. "Just checking the rest of the paperwork."

He moved around to the other side of his desk. Looking for a pencil and paper for me? He didn't have time for that. Nat wouldn't, and probably couldn't, wait on the phone much longer.

I waved at him again. This time I mimed throwing a punch.

"Here's the other report," Hart said. "Something about you arguing with a passenger over money. And it came to blows."

Oi. That wasn't exactly what I meant, nor was it what happened.

Radio silence filled the other end of the line.

We were going to lose him. I tried to imitate hugging some-one, but from the expression on Hart's face, I must have looked like I was having some sort of uncontrollable spasm. Good thing my pride had died long ago.

"I'm not trying to hang you out to dry, man," Hart said. "But my job's on the line if I don't check it out."

"I didn't hit him." Nat's voice had dropped to a whisper. He likely had someone else standing nearby. "I did yell at him. The guy's a cheat. He cheats people out of money for a living, and he cheats at cards. He didn't even need the money."

I cringed. Poor Carrie, hearing that about her husband. If someone had said something like that about Mark, I would have been jumping to his defense, even if it gave our presence away.

One good thing came from it, though. He'd said *is*. The guy *is* a cheater, present tense. That, along with his alibi for the window of opportunity, meant he wasn't our guy after all.

But one of the people at the poker game might still be.

I couldn't figure out a way to act out for Hart that I needed the other names.

I scooted over to his desk and opened a drawer. I grabbed out a pen.

He moved like he was going to stop me, afraid I was going to write on something official.

I scribbled *Ask for names* on the palm of my hand and held it up.

He nodded. "I need the names of the other people at the game to clear you."

"I'll text them to you." A short pause. "I gotta go. My next class starts in less than five minutes."

He hung up without waiting for Hart to tell him they were done.

Hart set the receiver in its cradle. "Why am I really getting that list from Nat? He couldn't have hurt Mr. Bodie, and we made up the part about someone reporting a fist fight."

He couldn't know for sure that there wasn't a fistfight at Nat's unsanctioned poker game. He must have guessed because Garth Bodie likely would have reported it much sooner had a staff member actually hit him.

The look on Carrie's face said she was wondering the same thing about the list, but she didn't want to undermine me by asking in front of Hart.

"Someone might have considered the verbal argument between Nat and Mr. Bodie as an opportunity to act against Mr. Bodie while also having a more likely suspect in place. If you could tell me when Nat provides you with the list—"

Hart pushed his hand toward me in a *stop* gesture. "I respect that your job is to look after the interests of the Bodies, but I can't give you access to names of our passengers or have you harassing them with questions. When Nat provides me with the list later tonight, I'll discretely talk to each of them and see if any of them even remembers the game in question, let alone knew Mr. Bodie well enough to know when his wife would be absent from their room." He stepped past us and opened the door. "Now, if you'll excuse me, it's late, and you've just dropped extra work on my desk."

Carrie's gaze darted between me and Hart. He was in the position of authority, and she clearly had the instinct to obey, but she'd also gotten used to me telling her what to do today.

Since arguing with him wouldn't get us access to the list, maybe it was time for me to step back. He'd done an okay job questioning Nat. Besides, if we left willingly, he might be more open to informing me if they came up with any leads.

And the bottom line was that I was on my honeymoon, with

a sick husband. If someone in an official position was going to investigate this instead of me needing to do it, I should let them.

I held out my hand to Hart. "Thank you for your help. We really appreciate it. It's reassuring to know that Mr. Bodie's disappearance is now being taken seriously."

Hopefully that was the right balance of gratitude, ego-stroking, and guilt-tripping to make sure he did, in fact, treat this like a missing person and follow up.

Carrie mimicked me by shaking Hart's hand, the shampoo and conditioner wedged into the crook of her other arm.

The expression on his face as we left looked like he thought he might have fallen into an alternate dimension. Either passengers rarely shook his hand or we'd come across as a touch crazy. Maybe a bit of both.

We walked in silence. I felt like throwing out the old *Penny for your thoughts?* cliché, but I was pretty sure I already knew where her thoughts were.

Halfway back to her cabin, Carrie slowed her steps. "You're kind of scary."

I stumbled even though the ship hadn't lurched. That was definitely not what I'd figured she was thinking. I'd been called a lot of things and accused of a lot of things, but *scary* hadn't appeared on the list until today. I wasn't even sure how to respond. My mom would have taken it as a compliment, but I wasn't my mom.

"I guess that helps when you're a lawyer." Carrie hugged the toiletries to her chest. "So what do we do now?"

We didn't do anything. *I* had to figure out a way to weasel information out of Hart once he talked to the people on the list. Considering I wasn't a police officer, and—as he'd pointed out—I had no authority on this ship, it was going to be difficult finding a legal way to do it.

"We should call Erik and Elise," Mark said once I explained what had happened. "They can look into Garth Bodie, and they might even be able to convince the security office to release the names of the people at the poker game to them."

I shifted positions so that I could use his chest as a pillow and listen to his heartbeat. We'd snuggled up together on the bed to talk. Mark hadn't wanted me to take the risk of catching what he had if it was a bug, but I didn't care. I wasn't going to assume we'd have a tomorrow. Carrie had gone off to exercise, thinking her husband would be there when she returned, and he hadn't been.

Life and our time together were going to pass by much quicker than I wanted them to. I wanted to be able to enjoy my job and help people. I also didn't want to look back on my life and regret that I hadn't spent more time with Mark. That was the balance that I didn't know how to find.

Mark jiggled his shoulder. "Have you fallen asleep on me?"

I grimaced against the fabric of his pajamas. "Sorry. No. You're right, but I hope I get Elise. I don't want the fifth degree from Erik about solving crimes on our honeymoon."

Mark chuckled. His chest sounded clear. I didn't hear any rattle or wheeze that I'd expect if he'd contracted pneumonia or something like that.

"You're still worrying about me, aren't you?" He spoke it more as a statement than a question.

"Maybe."

"You don't need to. This will pass, and we'll enjoy the rest of our trip together as soon as it does."

"Are you feeling any better?"

The fact that he didn't answer told me everything I needed to know. He hadn't improved. After I called Elise, I was going to do an Internet search for how long food poisoning could last.

THE CRUISE SHIP RAN ON PACIFIC STANDARD TIME BECAUSE IT departed from California, so I stayed up until three in the morning to be able to catch Elise, as she started work at six. I wanted to give her as much time as possible to look into things.

Elise's phone rang twice. "Scott."

Even though Elise had legally changed her last name after she married Erik, she still went by Elise Scott at work. They'd decided it would be too confusing having an Officer Higgins and a Sergeant Higgins working together.

I opened my mouth to respond, and a giant yawn came out instead.

"Nicole? Is that you?"

It said something that Elise recognized my yawn, but I was too tired to figure out what. "Sorry. I haven't had any sleep."

Elise let out a tiny snort. "Since you're married to my cousin, there are probably some things you shouldn't tell me about your wedded bliss."

Yarg. That was even more embarrassing than my game of charades in front of Hart earlier tonight...err, late last night. "You might wish that was why I wasn't sleeping once I tell you what's going on."

MY CELL PHONE RINGING WOKE ME UP. I GROPED AROUND IN THE dark for it. Maybe I shouldn't have gotten the plan that allowed me to make calls without astronomical roaming charges while we were out of the country. At this point, I was thinking we should have rented a remote cabin somewhere, even if it was cold and I had to cook.

Fair Haven Police Department flashed on the screen. Elise

must have found something and forgotten about the time difference despite my request that she hold off calling until after ten her time. According to my phone, it wasn't yet five in the morning my time. This was worse than jetlag.

I scooped up the phone and took it into the bathroom so my conversation wouldn't keep Mark awake.

"What did you find?" I asked, skipping the hello. She was doing me a favor, but even I couldn't be chipper at this time of the morning, on less than two hours' sleep.

"That you might, in fact, be a serial killer or a psychopath," Chief McTavish's voice answered back through the phone. "And that you still think this department is your own personal gophers."

The phone slipped in my grip. Oh crap. Elise had been caught. She'd been reprimanded before for using police resources to search into a case that didn't belong to her. This time she'd only done it because I'd begged. I should have known she'd get caught. Elise had the stealth tactics of a three-legged elephant.

"No normal person gets involved in a criminal case on their honeymoon," Chief McTavish continued. I had a feeling I'd already zoned out part of his tirade.

You'd have thought he'd cut me a little slack, considering I'd recently saved his life. Then again, McTavish didn't cut slack for anyone.

He did believe in justice, though. He also respected people who stood their ground when they were right. And I was right.

I tightened my grip on my phone. "A man disappeared on our cruise ship. His wife thinks something bad happened to him, and the security officers aren't treating it as a crime. What would you have done?"

His sigh was so loud I might have been able to hear it all the way out at sea without a phone. "Probably something like what you're doing, but with more respect for the proper authority."

I thought about sticking my tongue out at the phone, except that McTavish might have sensed it. His sixth sense wasn't as honed as my mom's, but it sometimes came close. "What would you have done differently?"

"I'd have called the agent I know with the FBI and passed it through his channels."

Even though we weren't in U.S. waters, the FBI would be the right ones to handle this. The cruise ship was registered with the U.S. and flew under a U.S. flag. However, a rogue call from some woman on a cruise ship wasn't likely to result in anyone looking into it quickly enough to catch who was behind this before the cruise ended.

"I don't have a contact at the FBI, and once this cruise is over, whoever did this will likely get away." I knew I was being cheeky, but if all McTavish was going to do was chew me out in the middle of the night, I was going back to bed.

"Given the mess your missing man was already in, I'm sure my contact will look into it. If we want him to prioritize this, though, I need to have the list of names from the poker game ready when I call him. There's no time and not enough evidence to get a warrant for them. He's not going to set aside what he's working on to look at this case if we can't show more proof than you currently have that something illegal went on."

McTavish and I often differed on what constituted enough evidence. It was likely because of our backgrounds. He felt the need to find evidence that someone like me couldn't pick apart in a courtroom with alternate explanations. I looked at evidence from the perspective of what would likely make a jury pass the point of reasonable doubt.

Wait. Had he said *already* in, not *is* in? "Something turned up in the search on Garth Bodie?"

"You could say that. He's been accused of mismanaging client funds for his own benefit. It's possible that someone on that list or a member of their family was financially screwed by Bodie and saw their chance for revenge."

If I had to make a guess, I would have said that that was exactly what happened to Garth. More than that, I had a feeling that one of the names on the list from the poker game would show a connection to him. It was possible he'd given them a chance to win some of their money and then had cheated at poker, costing them more. Or even won fairly. Either would have been rough to take.

Nat had accused Garth of cheating people out of their money in his job. That meant that at least some of the people at the private game knew what he did. Moreover, they knew he'd been accused of illegal activity within his job. That wasn't the kind of thing people tended to share, especially when participating in a game where money was on the line. Someone there must have known in advance.

"I'll get you the list today." Somehow.

"Try not to step on too many toes to do it," McTavish said.

That time I did stick my tongue out at the phone. At least he hadn't told me to do it legally. He knew I wouldn't cross those lines. Aside from the fact that anything we got illegally wouldn't be admissible in court, I didn't want to betray my faith by being unethical.

Since Hart wasn't likely to be in the security office at this time of night, I crawled back in bed, with the alarm on my phone set for seven. I was going to be a zombie tomorrow...minus the brain-eating part of course.

Honeymoons were supposed to be a restful time of bonding as husband and wife. Mark and I hadn't done anything the traditional way so far. Why start now?

WHEN I WALKED INTO THE SECURITY OFFICE RIGHT AFTER breakfast, Hart was leaned back in a chair, chugging coffee like he hadn't gotten much more sleep than I had. He'd probably been up all night, trying to decide whether or not he believed this was a criminal case.

His cheeks billowed out as if he were trying not to spit coffee across the room at the sight of me.

He swallowed down the gulp he'd just taken. "I haven't even started my day yet, let alone had time to speak to the guests who might have been at that game."

The way he phrased it was interesting. It sounded like he hadn't seen the list he asked Nat to text him. I'd been under the impression that he expected Nat to send him a list as soon as he finished his class. That might simply have been an assumption I made, though. My mind was too fuzzy from lack of sleep to remember exactly what'd been said.

I couldn't shake McTavish's admonition not to step on too many toes. The man was irritating. The last thing I wanted to do was prove him right. Rather than demanding to know if Nat had delivered the list, I'd come at it sideways. "Were there many names to follow up on?

He set his cup down. "Not many." He shifted his cup on the desk. "Is there anything else you needed?"

That shift of his cup seemed almost like a fidget. He didn't have a reason to be fidgety. We'd been here late last night, and I was back early this morning. As long as he had the list and planned to start speaking to the people on it today, he shouldn't have been nervous about my reaction.

Granted, it'd be uncomfortable to talk to guests about a potential altercation at a poker game that shouldn't have been taking place, but they hadn't done anything wrong. He wasn't putting them in any sort of compromising position by speaking to him.

So why was he reading as nervous?

Maybe it was just his personality. I hadn't noticed it last night, but it'd been late, and I'd been overly focused on the fact that I'd stormed into his office, holding shower products and wearing flip flops.

This morning I'd picked my most professional outfit. My parents would have suffered heart palpitations from hearing me describe my loose, flowy dress as *professional*, but it was the only dress—or close to dressy outfit—I had with me. We'd picked a casual cruise where it wasn't required to dress up for dinner, as we wanted to be able to relax completely. I hadn't packed anything I would normally wear to work.

But I needed him to take me seriously as a lawyer and not think of me as a passenger when I asked for the list. "Actually, there is one more thing. I spoke to a police contact of mine, and he'd like us to send him a copy of the list of names so he can cross-reference them for any prior connection with Mr. Bodie."

His desk seemed to jiggle slightly, almost as if his leg bounced. He crossed his arms over his chest. "I already told you that I can't give you a list of other passengers' names."

I couldn't quite get a read on whether he was annoyed or if his nervousness just amped up. He wasn't the straightforward person I'd assumed him to be at first.

I gave him my best impression of my mom's smooth-as-warm-butter smile, the one she used to convince someone it'd all been a misunderstanding when they started to get defensive. "You don't need to give it to me at all. You can send it straight to Chief McTavish."

Was it name-dropping if the person's name wouldn't be

immediately recognizable? Maybe more like title-dropping. Hopefully hearing I wanted him to send it to a police chief would erase any qualms.

He checked his watch. "I'm not sure if I have time for that right now."

Something was definitely wrong here. I couldn't put my finger on it. But it had to do with the list, and the fact that he didn't seem to want to send it to Chief McTavish any more than he wanted to show it to me.

I moved closer to his desk—close enough that I could have reached out and touched it. More often than I'd like to admit, the lessons my parents taught me came in handy. My dad used to say that the more someone balked, the more they were trying to hide. In this case, he was definitely hiding something about that list.

"I understand that you're busy, but my client won't. Hopefully you can understand that, too. Her husband is missing, after all. If you could just let me see the list, then I can reassure her that you have it and will send it to Chief McTavish for further investigation when you have a free minute."

He got to his feet.

I didn't want to show submission by backing up, but a little voice in the back of my head told me not to let him get between me and the door, regardless of what that cost me in negotiation ability. Too many people I hadn't thought would kill or harm had turned about to be exactly the person who'd committed the crime. I'd be stupid to assume Hart couldn't have been involved simply because he was a member of the security team.

From a logical perspective, a member of the security team was more likely to have been involved because they had access to areas of the ship that a normal passenger wouldn't, and no one would suspect them.

I stepped backward and to the side to make sure Hart couldn't easily get around me and block the door. "You *have* gotten the list, haven't you?"

Something flickered across his face. He opened his mouth, then shut it again. He retreated one step. "I don't have the list."

This could have all been a cover-up so that he wouldn't have to tell me he still wasn't taking this seriously. But that flicker of something that crossed his face made me think it was something deeper than that. He was afraid.

He hadn't sounded afraid of Nat on the phone. We'd been listening, so it could have been good acting. If he was that good of an actor, though, he should have been better at hiding the fact that he didn't have the list.

So maybe he was afraid of losing his job because he hadn't known an unsanctioned poker game was happening.

"All I'm interested in is finding out what happened to Garth Bodie." I kept my voice low and soft and coaxing, the same tone I used when my bullmastiff Toby tried to hide under the chairs at the veterinarian's office because he didn't want his shots. "I'm not interested in getting you in trouble."

I'd started to say *in trouble for anything unrelated to the case*, but then stopped myself. If he'd had something to do with the case, that phrasing would put him more on guard than he already was. I wanted to make him think that I wasn't suddenly concerned he might have had a part in this. Nothing good could come from tipping my hand at this point. I'd left Mark a note about where I'd gone, but look at how easily Garth had vanished. Hart could dispose of me and then claim I'd never made it here.

Hart leaned heavily against his desk as if his own weight were suddenly too much for him to support. "Nat knew I had no intention of checking out the names on the list. I don't need to. My name would have been on the list."

CHAPTER 8

I stared at Hart long enough that it almost crossed the line into awkward. My dad would have loved that announcement because it would have added evidence to his theory that no one was innocent. Ever.

"That's why you knew I made it up when I said there was a fight at the poker game." The words slipped from my thoughts and out of my lips before I could decide whether it was a good strategic move to speak them or not.

Hart's posture straightened slightly. "It tipped Nat off that someone else was listening in, too."

My estimation of Hart's caginess ratcheted up. Which also made me that much more cautious. I'd told him to ask about a fight—meaning an argument—and he'd pretended to misunderstand and asked instead about a physical fight in order to tip off the person we were talking to.

While I didn't think Hart was playing me now, I wasn't as confident as I might have been five minutes ago. He'd become an unreliable witness. I'd need to approach everything he told me with skepticism going forward. It also called into question what I'd heard on his call with Nat.

That said, he and Nat were still my best leads for who was at that game and might have wanted revenge on Garth Bodie.

Keeping up the I'm-Mr.-and-Mrs.-Bodie's-lawyer farce seemed to be the safest bet for now. By asking about other people, I might be able to bring Hart's guard down enough that he'd let something slip if he was hiding anything. "Did anyone else at the poker game seem to recognize Mr. Bodie?"

Hart's arms stiffened at his sides. I recognized it this time. He was getting ready to cover something up. "Not that I noticed."

That was an answer, but it wasn't. It was the kind of dodge that most people would miss if they weren't expecting the other person to lie to them. "How many people were there?"

A muscle twitched in the corner of Hart's eye. I got the feeling he was sizing me up.

He settled his weight soundly on both feet. "Who are you really? Are you a cop?"

The shift in posture was a bit startling. He'd still been playing me before—or trying to. First, he'd been the lackadaisical security officer who didn't think anything had actually happened to Garth. Then he was the guilty, ashamed security officer who was afraid of losing his job because he liked to gamble on the side.

Now, for the first time, it felt like I was seeing the real Hart. Now that the masks were off, it was time to play it straight.

I changed my posture to match—shoulders back and chin up the way my mom had taught me. "I'm who I said I am, but I'm a criminal defense attorney. I met the Bodies on this cruise, and Mrs. Bodie asked me to represent her when her husband disappeared. She's afraid his family will try to blame her."

The skin at the corner of Hart's eyes tightened. "Are you here looking for a strawman?"

In other words, was I looking to pin this on him because my client was guilty of doing something to her husband? "I'm looking for the truth."

He didn't move a muscle in his body. Even the twitch next to his eye had stopped. "The truth is that Garth Bodie is exactly what Nat said he was—a cheat."

For the first time, I believed he was telling me the complete truth. The question was what I did with that truth and how it could help us figure out what had really happened. "How do you know?"

"I recognized him as the man who cheated my mom out of her life savings with his shady investment schemes."

I would have been excited by the fact that I had the self-control not to cringe if it hadn't been for the other fact that Hart's admission made my body feel heavy, like an entire pool full of water was crushing down on me. To lose everything and have to figure out how to support yourself when you should be retiring was a scary situation. "I'm really sorry."

Hart shook his head and moved around to the backside of his desk. He lowered himself slowly into his chair. "Nat's my first cousin. I got him the job here. When I figured out who Bodie was, I asked him to help me. I'd read somewhere that Bodie liked to gamble, and Nat put himself through school by playing professional poker. We thought we could win back at least some of what my mom lost."

I didn't need Hart to fill in the rest of the blanks for me. They'd invited Garth Bodie to a private poker game. Maybe they'd filled it out with a few friends they could trust. Maybe it'd just been the three of them. I didn't know exactly how many people were required to play poker. My parents felt that gambling was one of the highest vices. They didn't like leaving anything up to chance.

Regardless, Bodie had accepted and then cheated at the game, taking their money, too. It'd have had to be a high-stakes game if they wanted to win back their family member's life savings. They might have even borrowed the money or taken a loan on their credit cards to be able to do it.

And if Nat had played professional poker for a while, he'd have recognized a cheater when he saw one.

It provided a huge motive for them to have killed Garth.

Sort of. Killing him might have made them feel vindicated

for the moment, but it wouldn't have gotten them their money back. Or Hart's mom's money back.

If they were involved, this was more likely a kidnapping for ransom. It was their next logical step to get their money back, assuming you could call any criminal activity logical.

If I was right, it meant Garth's chances of being alive just went up by a huge leap. It also meant we either had to figure out how to find where they'd hidden him on the ship, or we had to find a way to prove that Hart and Nat sent the ransom demand once it arrived.

I thanked Hart for being honest with me and lied to him that we'd be crossing him and Nat off our list of suspects. To add even more credence to my lie, I asked him to continue searching the ship for Garth. I was a criminal lawyer, but Carrie could hire someone else to sue the cruise line and so on.

My parents had taught me well how to play a suspect, and I was decent at it—though maybe that wasn't something I should brag about.

Hart seemed to believe me. Granted, he'd also lied to me before, and I couldn't be sure he wasn't playing me in return. Even if he was, we were now playing a waiting game to see if a note arrived.

After I filled Mark in and texted McTavish to investigate both Nat and Hart, I spent the rest of the morning snuggled up with Mark, doing crosswords. The mental puzzle seemed to distract him from how ill he felt—as did rehashing what we'd learned so far about Garth and what it all might mean.

It wasn't what we'd planned for our honeymoon, but it didn't matter. At least we were together.

I'd ordered us room service for lunch, since Mark felt like eating, when my phone dinged.

I need you, Carrie had written. *Please come.*

Mark read the message over my shoulder. "They've either found Garth's body, or your theory is right and the kidnappers sent a ransom note. Either way, you should go."

I kissed him. I didn't know yet how to balance being a good wife and working cases, but it somehow felt wrong leaving him here. "Are you sure?"

He smiled just enough that his dimples peeked out. "You can't back out now. You'd only make McTavish angrier."

He had a point. I texted Carrie to let her know I was on my way and hurried to her room.

She stood in the doorway, waiting for me, one foot propping her door open and a note in her hand.

She held the note out toward me by two fingers, as if she were afraid it might be carrying anthrax.

I took it from her, holding it carefully between my thumb and index finger as well so I'd destroy as few fingerprints as possible, if there were any.

Fingerprints on paper were one of the hardest to make visible. Only around half of the prints on a piece of paper could be made sufficiently visible for a clear print identification because prints on paper depended on how well the particular type of paper absorbed the sweat from a person's fingers. Nanotech-nology was making strides in improving fingerprint extraction from paper, but it wasn't widely in use yet. I didn't want to risk destroying whatever good prints might be there.

I entered Carrie's cabin and laid the paper down on the desk. The letter was typed, so the chances that the paper had prints on it were slim. A sender who took the time to type a note usually also took the precaution of wearing gloves.

If you want to see your husband again, it read, *get off at the next port of call and don't get back on the ship. We'll be in touch.*

I leaned back from the desk. It was the ransom note I'd been expecting—and somewhat hoping—for. And yet it wasn't.

It didn't ask for a specific amount of money. It didn't give her a timeline in which to get the money or a place to drop it.

It was the vaguest ransom letter I'd ever heard of.

Carrie wrapped her arms around her barely covered midriff. "That means he's still alive, right? They want me to get off the ship and pay some money and then they'll return him."

Probably. Possibly, anyway. But something about it wasn't sitting right with me. "They didn't even tell you where to go once you left the ship. How will they know how to contact you again?"

Carrie shook her head so hard that a few tendrils of hair escaped from her ponytail. "It doesn't matter. I have to do it. If he's alive and I don't, they might kill him."

Of course she'd pick now to start making decisions on her own. I recognized the granite tone to her voice. It was the one that said *I can't lose him*. It was the one that said *He's worth the risk*. It was one I was familiar with because I felt the same way about Mark.

Suddenly, all I wanted to do was get back to our cabin and hold onto Mark tightly and not let go.

I swallowed hard. Mark wasn't in imminent danger. Carrie was. Not every place in South America was safe.

When my dad learned that Mark and I wanted to honeymoon somewhere warm, he forbade us from going to Mexico, citing kidnapping statistics and the story of a woman who was shot in Mexico City while on her honeymoon. Mexico had never been on my list. To make him feel like we were doing what he wanted, though, we told him we'd take a cruise to South America instead.

Our plan backfired. South America, according to him, was a place where criminals like Robert Vesco settled after embezzling their millions. My mom placated him by making a list of the safest stops in South America for tourists and vetting our cruise before we booked. She'd "helped" us select the cruise that stopped at the fewest risky locations. Mark had joked that he hadn't realized planning our honeymoon would be more of a family affair than planning our wedding had been.

It'd been funny at the time, but thanks to my parents, I knew too much about what cities were safe and what cities weren't. If Carrie got off at the next port of call, she'd be in one of the cities where only a few select areas were safe. She wouldn't know where those were. And she'd be easy prey for anyone who decided they wanted something from a young, female non-local.

The danger might be worth it if we could be sure they'd return Garth once she did what they asked. I wasn't sure they would. I had to convince her not to go. Every survival instinct I had said she'd never be seen again if she did.

I stepped aside so Carrie could see the note again if she wanted to. "Their request doesn't make sense. If they wanted money for ransom, you'd be better able to get it onboard the ship or when we return to American soil. They might be trying to lure you off the ship to kidnap you as well or to make you look guilty for Garth's disappearance."

She snatched the letter from the desk. "I called you here to help me."

She might call it *help*, but it was looking like she'd actually called me here for moral support. She didn't want help making the decision about what to do. She'd already made it. There wasn't anything I could do other than help her pack her bags if she'd already decided to leave the ship when it docked.

It was the same thing she'd done when she claimed to need a

lawyer. She hadn't needed a lawyer. She'd just wanted someone by her side when she made the decision to call security.

I wasn't going to back up her decision this time.

A cold tingle made my fingers go numb. There was one other reason she might have called me here.

She might have called me here to have a witness to the note. The only reason she'd need to do that, though, was if she had actually hurt Garth, and now she wanted to be able to disappear and still be thought innocent.

I'd be the perfect witness if she wanted that. I was a lawyer, and I had nothing personal to gain from Garth's death or her disappearance. If anyone questioned it, even money couldn't be a motive for me to lie. My bank accounts wouldn't show any strange deposits.

There was one person I hadn't had McTavish look into.

Carrie.

In case my suspicions were wrong, I needed to try one more time to convince her not to leave the ship.

"If they want a ransom for Garth, you have more leverage than you think. We can tell them you'll get them the money, but that you'll only do it from the ship."

"We don't know who sent the note. We can't ask them anything." She crumpled the letter up and tossed it into the trash can, destroying any potential fingerprints. "I'm tired. I think you need to leave now. I don't want to have to call security again."

If she wasn't listening to logic, she wouldn't have any qualms about calling security on me. Hart would probably love to toss me out after the position I'd put him in.

I made eye contact. "Please think about what I said."

She didn't reply. Instead, she directed a stare at the door.

I let myself out. I had to leave, but I didn't have to give up. At this point, I couldn't give up and live at peace with myself. Because one of two things was going to happen—either the person who hurt Garth was also going to hurt Carrie, or Carrie was a murderer about to walk away free with all of her new husband's money.

CHAPTER 10

I headed back to our cabin, texting Chief McTavish Carrie's name along the way.

Married name or maiden name? he wrote back almost instantly.

Crap. I didn't know Carrie's maiden name. She was going by Bodie because they were married, but she wouldn't have had time to legally change her name yet. And with the interaction we'd just had, she wasn't about to tell me her maiden name or even let me back into her cabin to snoop around and look for her passport.

That left me with one option if I wanted McTavish to poke into her background. I'd have to get her last name from the ship's passenger manifest. Since I didn't have access to it myself, that meant asking a crew member to give it to me.

Unfortunately for me, the only crew member who wouldn't

look at me like I'd had too much to drink simply for asking was Hart.

Not only was he also a suspect, but he'd made it clear that he wasn't going to hand over passengers' names to me. Though, technically, he hadn't been willing to hand over other passengers' names. He might be willing, maybe, to give me Carrie's actual last name.

I stopped my march down the hallway. If I was going to the security office instead of our cabin, I needed to take a left.

I just wasn't sure if I should. It came down to who I trusted least at this point—Carrie or Hart.

In the past, I would have made my choice and run off after it, but I wasn't a single person anymore. Everything I did now affected someone else.

I dialed Mark's cell phone.

"Did you forget how to get back to our room again?" There was a smile in his voice even though he still sounded worn-out.

I'd only forgotten a few times. When we'd originally found our room, I hadn't planned to need to ever find it without Mark. "I have a slightly bigger dilemma."

I filled him in on what happened. "So either way, we can't let her get off this ship, but the only way to stop her is to figure out what really happened to Garth."

"Within the next twenty-four hours."

The ship would be getting into port tonight. The announcement at breakfast had said no one would be allowed to disembark due to the late arrival time, but that excursions would begin as scheduled the next morning. "More like twelve, and McTavish isn't going to want to stay up all night."

"So let's run it down," Mark said. "If it's Carrie, then the smartest move is to go to Hart and get his help. She can't be allowed off the ship. There'll be no finding her once she leaves."

I checked the hallway to make sure no one was coming down it from either direction at the moment. "If it's Hart, then the worst he's going to do is try to delay me because he wants Carrie to leave the ship. I won't be a threat to him if his goal was to point suspicion at her. He'll actually be happy I'm doing it."

Which, thankfully, also meant I wouldn't be in danger from Hart. I'd only be in danger from him if I continued investigating him as a suspect.

"You don't think he's behind this anymore?"

"He might still be, but he'd only have one of two goals at this point. He'd either want money from Carrie, in which case I think he'd have sent a traditional ransom demand. Or he'd be afraid enough that I'm on to him and Nat that he wanted to divert suspicion."

Even if someone else sent the note, they likely weren't planning to leave the ship themselves. They had no reason to. We currently had few leads. Once Carrie left the ship and didn't return, anyone who cared enough to notice would either think they'd disappeared together or that Carrie had killed Garth and fled.

A couple approached from down the hall. I asked Mark to hang on and waited for them to pass by. The halls always made me think of the below-deck areas shown in the movie *Titanic*. They were narrow enough that I had to press against the handrail because the woman didn't want to release the man's hand as they passed.

I waited until they were far enough away that I was sure they wouldn't hear me. "What do you think I should do?"

In the pause that followed, I could imagine Mark running the probabilities in his head. How likely was it that going there alone would put me in a dangerous situation?

"You should go to Hart," he said. "Tell him about the note, and ask him to give you Carrie's last name."

I started to move the phone away to disconnect, but Mark wasn't done.

"And if you're not back or I haven't heard from you in twenty minutes, I'm sounding a fire alarm."

Even though it would mean evacuating the entire boat and probably getting arrested for tampering with safety equipment, I knew he'd do it if it meant keeping me safe.

HART WAS STILL IN HIS OFFICE. A FEMALE OFFICER WHO WORE her ponytail a little too high and tight to be comfortable and two other male officers closer to fifty than to my age stood in a semi-circle around him, almost blocking him from my view.

They were going over something together on the desk, and they didn't seem to notice when I entered. I rapped my knuckles lightly on the edge of the door.

Hart glanced up, then looked back up again as if my face hadn't fully registered the first time.

If an expression ever said *oh crap*, his did. He hadn't been expecting me.

That could mean either of two things. It could mean he'd sent the note and he thought I'd figured it out, or it could mean he hadn't sent the note and so he thought our conversation this morning would have gotten me out of his hair for longer than a few hours.

It'd be nice if people came with motivation subtitles.

Hart swept the pages on his desk together and handed them to the female officer. "We'll go over the rest of the security reports later. Go back to your rounds for now."

I stepped out of the way. The male officers didn't even glance at me on the way by, as if they'd become immune to whatever crazy thing would happen next on the ship. The female officer had that I'm-curious-but-I'm-trying-not-to-show-it look written all over her.

Since I knew what happened when I got curious, I was never entirely comfortable when someone else was. For all I knew, she'd have her own reasons to suspect Hart of wrongdoing, and she'd be investigating me next.

They all exited, and I glared at the door. It had no way of locking it to make sure someone wasn't going to walk in on us. In fact, it was probably thin enough that anyone serious about eavesdropping would be able to without needing any fancy equipment or help.

Hopefully Hart wouldn't be thinking the same thing. He'd never give me Carrie's last name if he suspected we might be overheard. Even though he'd be sending it to a police chief, his job could still be on the line depending on the cruise company's privacy policies. They didn't have to release passenger's names without a warrant. In fact, I was sure the powers-that-be would refuse to release any information without a warrant.

"You ever hear the saying about the bad penny," Hart said.

I'd take the showing up at an inopportune time part of that reference, and I was probably unwanted, but…okay, he had used that in a way I couldn't argue with.

Given that he saw me that way, I'd need to be cagey in how I approached this. "I know we agreed that there was no need to send the list of names from the poker game to my police contact." That wasn't entirely a lie. I hadn't sent McTavish a list per se. I'd simply given him two names of people I knew had a grudge against Garth Bodie. "But I do need your help with something else."

He looked for a second like he wanted to tell me that he had important work to do—real work. He looked like he wanted to, but he didn't, probably because I still knew something he didn't want his employers to find out. That did give me a bit of a negotiating advantage.

He stared at me with his eyebrows raised, waiting.

"I'm not convinced anymore that Carrie wasn't involved in the disappearance of her husband. I need her maiden name so I can have my police contact run a background check on her."

Hart had been leaning on his desk. He pushed away from it now. "I'm glad you're not my lawyer, if you swap sides that easily."

Ouch. I didn't see it as swapping sides. I saw it as being on the side of truth and justice from start to finish. "I only defend innocent clients. Carrie knows that."

"And what makes you think she might not be innocent?"

It felt like he was fishing for information. That was okay by me. I wanted him to think he was no longer a suspect. Not only would that increase my chances of him helping me investigate Carrie, but it'd also take his guard down and increase his chances of screwing up.

I told him about the note and how she was insistent about leaving the ship and waiting for whoever sent it to contact her.

His eyes narrowed slightly at the edges, a micro-tell that he couldn't control. Like he suspected I was trying to trick him. "That's a funny reason to suspect she's behind her husband's disappearance. Receiving a ransom note would make me think someone else kidnapped her husband for money."

I met his gaze without blinking. "They didn't ask for money, didn't tell her where to go, and didn't say how they'd get back into contact with her."

He nodded his head in such slow motion that it almost felt like he was trying to buy himself time to think. "That does sound staged," he said, equally slowly.

Something was definitely brewing in his mind, but I wasn't sure what. It could be that he'd sent the note. But if he had, he should have been glad I was looking somewhere else. Though perhaps he wasn't glad despite that because I'd figured out that the person who sent the note wasn't after money at all.

I wanted to stomp my foot. This case was tangled up into more knots than if I'd tried to take the knot-tying class the cruise ship offered as a free activity during our days at sea.

Hart pressed the knuckles of one hand into the top of his desk and leaned his weight on that arm. "So you want Carrie Bodie's legal name so that you can see if she'd been involved in anything suspicious in the past."

I nodded and tried not to imagine what he must be thinking about the fact that I'd taken on a client without knowing her real last name. In my silent defense, it wasn't like I'd intended to have to defend her. In fact, I hadn't intended to become this mixed up in the case on my own honeymoon. If Mark hadn't been so sick and cabin-bound, we might not be in this position at all.

Hart shifted his weight back off his arm and tapped his knuckles lightly on the desk. I could almost see his mental ledger making calculations. Was it better to keep me off his trail by giving me what I needed to investigate Carrie? Or was it better to not risk his job by giving me passenger information? For all he knew, I wasn't looking into Carrie at all, and I planned to use his breach of confidentiality against him to get him investigated more closely.

If that's the path his mind was headed down—and I suspected it was—I needed to set him at ease. "I'm still Carrie's legal counsel. Giving me her last name doesn't breach any privacy laws. You'd have a strong case for it being the right thing to confirm for me that I have her name correct."

His eyes did that slight narrowing at the edges again. "I'll look it up for you, but then I need you to stop showing up at my office unannounced. I have other work to do. I can't keep helping you chase down a man who no one wants found anyway. If you're right about his wife, she just made sure she's never going to have to think about money for the rest of her life, even if she bathes in diamonds and eats three squares a day of truffles and caviar."

I sent Carrie's legal last name—Donovan—to Chief McTavish, but it was late enough his time that he didn't know if he'd be able to get back to me before morning. As much as I hated to do it, I told him to contact me as soon as he found anything out, regardless of what time it was for me. The ship would be docking tonight, and excursions started tomorrow morning at eight.

That meant that, if I couldn't stop her by seven fifty-nine tomorrow morning, Carrie would get off the ship and likely never be heard from again.

I turned my phone's notification volume up as loud as it would go before settling in to bed. Even though it would wake up Mark, I couldn't take the risk of missing Chief McTavish's call because I slept through it. With how tired I felt, I pretty much needed the phone to be fire-alarm loud.

I must have drifted off almost immediately. The next thing I knew, I jerked awake from a nightmare where Carrie and Hart were fighting over who would get to throw me overboard. The blankets had tangled around my legs, and my Bible lay flopped open on the bed beside me where it must have fallen. Mark had turned off the over-the-bed light at some point.

The red numbers of the bedside clock glowed so brightly my eyes blinked instinctively. Two in the morning. Too early for Chief McTavish to be calling. My dream must have woken me up.

I closed my eyes.

My phone beeped with a text notification. It was probably the follow-up notification, and the first one was what woke me.

But it was the middle of the night pretty much everywhere right now. It was probably some sort of automated text from my cell phone company telling me about updates.

They didn't normally text that sort of thing in the middle of the night, though. Their customers would get annoyed awfully fast if that was standard practice.

I ought to check my phone just in case.

I groped around on my bedside table, bumped my phone, and knocked it to the floor. It hit the deck with a cringe-worthy thunk. It'd be par for the course for this trip if I also broke my phone.

My body was so tired that, even as I told it to lean over and reach for the phone, all it wanted to do was go back to sleep. There couldn't be anything important anyone would be texting me about right now. Anything important would merit a phone call.

I squinted over the side of the bed. My phone had landed face up, glowing up at me.

The message looked like it was from Carrie Bodie, but I couldn't be sure from this distance. Whoever it was from, there wasn't much to the text. A letter or two at most.

A bit of the grogginess left my system.

I leaned over the side of the bed and fished my phone off the floor. The text read *He*. The three flashing dots that said she was writing another message blinked below it. She must have hit the Send icon too soon.

I shifted back in bed to wait. Whatever it was better be important, like she'd been trying to type *He's back* and Garth interrupted her with an affectionate embrace.

The dots kept flashing. A minute passed. Then two.

The sleepiness drained from my body and collected into a heavy lump in my stomach. She obviously knew she'd sent me the first text. In the middle of the night. Even if Garth had returned, she should have been able to take the time to finish.

Unless she couldn't.

He could also be the start of *Help*.

"Mark." I slid out of bed and hit the lights. "Call security to Carrie's room."

"What?" his voice was groggy.

I had to find my running shoes. I couldn't move fast enough in flip flops, and I'd already wasted a lot of time. Assuming I was right and she was in trouble. I might be over-reacting.

It wasn't a risk I was willing to take. Forget the shoes. Forget the fact that I'd have to run down public cruise ship corridors barefoot. I had to go.

Mark was sitting up now, reaching for his phone. "What time is it?"

"Late. Early. I got a weird text from Carrie." I headed for the door. "Send security or whatever staff you can reach to her room."

I didn't wait to see if Mark would do it. I knew he would, if for no other reason than I was running off in my pajamas in the middle of the night. Thank goodness I slept in shorts and a t-shirt rather than a lacy nightgown.

I sprinted out the door and down the hall. At least I'd been to Carrie's room enough times to keep from getting lost.

My lungs and thighs burned before I was halfway there, and I tripped going up the flights of stairs between her deck and mine. I didn't dare look at my toes. From the warm, throbbing feeling, I was certain at least one of them was bleeding. If I looked down, there was a good chance I might pass out.

I burst out the stairwell door. The slow-close mechanism was the only thing that kept it from hitting the wall and bouncing back at me hard enough to knock me down the stairs.

The hallway was as bright as it was in the daytime. Much like a hotel, the cruise ship never turned down the corridor lights, probably for security reasons.

I jog-limped for Carrie's cabin.

Her cabin door swung open, and a man backed out. Not just a man. Hart.

I froze.

He hauled a woman along with him, one arm looped around her waist. It had to be Carrie, but she leaned on him awkwardly, as if she couldn't support her own weight. Her steps were a clumsy imitation of her usual movement.

Dear Lord, he'd drugged her somehow. She was so trusting that she would have let him into her room without wondering why a security officer needed to visit her in the middle of the night. It would have been easy enough for him to come up with some story about Garth to get her to let him in even if she had questioned it.

She must have tried to text me when she realized he'd given her something to drug her. The state of her room would tell whether or not there'd been a struggle over her cell phone once he figured out what she was trying to do. My guess was that whatever he'd spiked her drink with hadn't kicked in enough for her to hand over the phone easily. She may have even gotten it back at some point and tried to send me a second text.

Since Hart was ship's security, I would have been the only one she felt she could trust. She'd probably tried to text me without him seeing it.

Mark would have help on the way soon, but I couldn't let them leave this floor. As soon as they did, the cavalry wouldn't know where to find us. Hart could drag her off into the bowels of the ship or throw her overboard or whatever he planned to do before anyone could stop him.

"Hart." I'd intended to call his name loudly and forcefully, but my voice came out a little cracked around the edges. Not unlike my sanity. Maybe McTavish was right. Something was very wrong with me that I kept ending up in situations like this—and on my honeymoon no less. "Stop."

Surprisingly, he did. No doubt he hadn't planned for someone who knew him and Carrie to find them. If a random passenger had spotted them, he could have made up some story about her being sick or drunk and he was taking her to the infirmary.

He turned them around.

Carrie blinked rapidly, like she was trying to focus, and reached a hand halfway in my direction. "Dizzy."

Her voice was so soft I might have thought I'd imagined it had I not seen her lips move.

"I know you are." I forced myself to walk down the hall toward them as if I wasn't afraid of Hart at all. At least he couldn't see the way my insides felt like they were sloshing around in a paint shaker. "You need to turn her over to me, Rick."

I sent up a quick prayer that I'd remembered his first name correctly. I'd only heard it the one time when he was on the phone with Nat. But I needed to forge some sort of bridge to stall him at worst and at best get him to give up on whatever plan he had and turn himself in once someone official came.

"I can't do that." His expression reminded me of concrete hardening in the sun. "I also can't let her get off this ship. She leaves the ship, and we'll never get my mom's money back."

What the...? I don't know what I expected him to say, but

that wasn't it. He was here because I'd told him about the note instructing Carrie to leave the ship. Which meant he hadn't sent the note. He didn't want her to leave the ship, either.

I moved another step closer. Hopefully Carrie would understand that, whatever I said, I didn't plan to let him leave this floor with her in tow. "I want everyone to get what they need here. How will taking her anywhere get your mom's money back?"

Hart dragged Carrie a step toward the elevator. "When her husband shows back up, he'll have to pay to get her back."

I edged along with him. Hart couldn't have been the one to take Garth if he expected Garth to be returned and pay a ransom for Carrie. The note must have given him an idea for a new way he could get his mom's life savings back. "And if her husband doesn't come back? Then what?"

He tightened his hold on Carrie. She squeaked.

"Then she'll tell whatever banker controls their funds to pay up. Either way, my mom gets back what's rightfully hers, and so does Nat. He shouldn't have to suffer because he wanted to help me out."

It sounded like my guess had been right. Whatever Hart and Nat lost in the poker game with Garth, they'd overextended themselves to get it.

Hart's plan might have worked if Carrie hadn't sent that text.

He'd almost dragged her all the way back to the elevator now.

"I've already told my husband what's going on," I said, "and security—other security—will be here any second. It'd be better for you if you'd already let Carrie go by the time they get here."

The elevator door dinged open. For a second, I thought Hart had managed to press the button when I wasn't looking.

Hart swung Carrie around, putting her between himself and the elevator almost like he planned to use her as a shield, his arm snaked around her neck.

The young security guard with the high-and-tight military haircut stepped out of the elevator. "I heard what she said, Rick. She's right. I can't let you leave with her, but I'd like to be able to tell the captain that you let her go willingly."

Hart dropped his hold on Carrie. Her legs buckled, and I leaped forward. I wasn't in time to catch her. It was more like I cushioned her as she fell. Her elbow connected with my ribs on the way down. That was going to leave yet another bruise.

After asking me if I could get Carrie to the infirmary and then return to the security office, the other security officer led Hart off.

"Make him give Garth back, too," Carrie slurred. She fisted the edge of my long t-shirt in her hand. "Make him."

Tears dripped down her cheeks.

I didn't even have a tissue to help dab them away. "I don't think he has Garth, sweetie."

She leaned against me. "I didn't even want to go on a cruise for our honeymoon. Why wouldn't Garth listen?"

Taking a cruise for their honeymoon hadn't actually caused

what happened. Unfortunately, Carrie might not have been willing to acknowledge that even if she hadn't been drugged. She needed someone or something to blame.

Her reaction also made me think I'd still been looking in the wrong direction for who made Garth vanish. Hart clearly hadn't done it. But Carrie was too drugged to be coherent enough to lie to me.

Somewhere on this ship still hid the person behind all of this.

By the time I passed Carrie into the care of a nurse and made it to the security office, both the captain and Mark were there. The captain had the distinct look of someone who'd been forced out of bed into looking professional when he wasn't ready to be awake. He'd missed a button on his jacket.

Mark wore shorts and a t-shirt, but also the look of a man who was used to being hauled out of bed in the middle of the night. His ability to be ready whenever a crisis hit made me want to kiss him. It let me know he'd always be there for me as long as it was within his power. He was probably the most awake of the three of us, even though I'd been the one to sprint down the corridors.

Not only was he out of bed, but he also looked distinctly less pasty than the last time I saw him. "You look better." I flinched. Maybe that wasn't the nicest way to phrase it. "I mean, you look like you're feeling better."

His lips tilted up at one side. "We might have been premature in assuming it wasn't seasickness. I got turned around on my way to the security office—"

I held up a hand, stopping him. "Wait." I couldn't keep the laugh out of my voice, despite the late hour and the circumstances. "You mean *you* got lost."

Mark gave me an I'm-not-amused eyebrow raise, but the other side of his mouth lifted as well, revealing his dimples and giving him away. "Unlike you, I've been in our cabin the whole time. But yes, I took a wrong turn." He emphasized *wrong turn* rather than using the actual word *lost*. "No one answered at the security office when I called. I called the concierge desk, and the woman must have thought I was playing a prank because she told me to call back in the morning. I ended up wandering around above deck until I found a security officer on rounds."

Which explained why it took him so long to send help, but not why he was now sure he was seasick. Except... "You never went below deck on my parents' boat."

"Nope."

For two people who helped solve crimes for a living, we'd made a hasty assumption without enough evidence. Mark could have been feeling better this whole time if we'd gotten a cabin with an ocean view, if he'd spent his days on the deck, or if he'd even gone to the infirmary for a seasickness shot. Well, at least we'd be able to enjoy the rest of our trip.

Sort of. We still had the issue of Hart and a missing man to deal with.

The captain cleared his throat, probably tired of waiting for us. Even though we hadn't had a normal honeymoon so far, we couldn't be blamed for having a moment of honeymoon euphoria where we were so wrapped up in each other that we almost forgot about everything else. We *were* newlyweds, after all.

The captain ran a hand down the front of his shirt. He must have felt the undone button because his hand stopped overtop of it. "We're not equipped to handle serious crimes."

I wouldn't have expected them to be. Cruise ships weren't built with brigs. The way his hand stayed over his undone button made me think he might be more worried about appearances, though. "Your cruise line has a very positive rating online. We know this isn't the norm."

His hand edged down slightly. "I'm going to have to account for all of this to corporate. Once this hits the news, they're going to want to issue a press release saying that a two-time kidnapper was apprehended and handed over to authorities immediately." His hand moved down into his lap as if he'd given up on trying to hide the rogue button. "I know Rick Hart. He manages his department well. I have a hard time believing he kidnapped one person and tried to kidnap another, and I certainly don't want to hand him over to officials in a foreign country."

We were docked at a South American port. We weren't at sea any longer. It was an area where the law got fuzzy and application got even fuzzier.

Knowing what I knew of Hart's motives, I didn't want to see him handed over to foreign police, either. I didn't know whether countries in South America even had due process. Maybe it made me an egocentric American for thinking it, but I happened to believe we had one of the best justice systems in the world and that Americans should be able to avail themselves of their right to a fair trial and innocence until proven guilty.

"We're docked now, but the crimes were committed while we were out at sea. Since this ship sails under an American flag, you can tell corporate that the United States has jurisdiction and that you can't hand Hart over to anyone else."

"I'll tell them that. Thank you." The captain rose to his feet. "I'll need you both to fill out incident reports in the morning for CYA purposes, but it doesn't have to be first thing. I know it's late, and you've been through a lot."

Mark stood and shook the man's hand.

I stayed seated. Hart was in custody, but I was close to certain that he wasn't behind Garth's disappearance. That created an additional problem. "There's one more thing."

Both Mark and the captain turned to look at me. From the way Mark tensed slightly, I had a guess that he knew what was coming and was bracing for the captain's reaction.

"You need to cancel excursions for tomorrow," I said, "and keep everyone on the ship."

The captain buttoned the button that had been undone. Forcefully. "There's no need for us to be excessive about this. We have the person behind all the trouble under house arrest. He won't be able to sneak off the ship tomorrow."

My brain calculated whether it was better for me to stay seated as a sign that we weren't leaving until this was resolved or to stand to place myself on the level of his equal. Given that I was wearing my pajamas and no shoes, standing up probably wouldn't have that much of an impact. It'd only draw more attention to my appearance.

I did raise my gaze to meet his. "Rick Hart did try to kidnap Carrie Bodie, but I don't believe he's the one behind Mr. Bodie's disappearance. He seemed to think he'd be able to ransom Carrie and that Mr. Bodie would willingly pay once he was found. To me, that doesn't sound like a man who knows where Mr. Bodie is."

"You want me to believe there are two kidnappers on my ship?" The captain's voice said he thought he might be being punished for something.

It did sound ludicrous when he put it so bluntly. I hadn't

come this far and sacrificed so much of my honeymoon to back down, though—pajamas or no pajamas. "I believe that's the way the facts point. If you allow excursions tomorrow, you'll be giving the second kidnapper a chance to escape the ship."

The way he narrowed his lips and tilted backward onto his heels let me know he thought I was unreasonable rather than logical. He might not have phrased it that way. I was still a paying passenger, after all.

Paying passenger or not, he wasn't going to acquiesce to my request. I could see it in his body language.

My dad would say I shouldn't be making a request.

I glanced at Mark. He wasn't stopping me. I was going to take that as support, if not agreement.

"The kidnappings have already been brought to the attention of a chief of police and an FBI agent. They agree with my assessment of the situation." Or I was sure they would once I had a chance to update McTavish. My sleep-groggy brain couldn't actually remember if McTavish had already talked to his contact or not, but it sounded good. "I'm certain 'corporate' would rather you closed down the ship and they had to refund everyone their money than the PR nightmare they'll have on their hands when it comes out that you didn't lock the ship down after you were informed that there were concerns that Rick Hart hadn't taken part in the first disappearance."

The captain's nod looked like someone had tugged on his

hair, but at least it was agreement. "I'll talk to head office tonight to try to secure their approval."

It wasn't a promise, but it was as close as we were going to get.

During breakfast, the captain himself made the announcement that, due to circumstances beyond the ship's control, shore excursions were canceled and they'd be turning around for the U.S. immediately.

"Where the FBI will probably meet the ship and need to clear everyone before they disembark," Mark whispered.

I had no doubt of it. Turning the ship around meant they'd also be providing all the passengers with vouchers for a future trip to reimburse them for this one. The people in charge must have consulted with their media and legal departments and realized that would be a smaller loss than the press crapstorm they'd face if they didn't approach this seriously enough, possibly because they'd looked up my name and my parents' law firm popped up. They may have even thought we'd be defending Hart and that we'd cast a negative light on the cruise line if they left any opportunities for us to do so in defense of a client.

I leaned closer to Mark. "I'm sorry we won't be able to finish the trip now that you're feeling better. I feel responsible."

Mark shoveled another huge forkful of eggs into his mouth. "You didn't kidnap or kill anyone. You didn't cause this."

I hadn't. True. It wasn't that so much as the part I'd played in the whole scenario and what it'd meant for our honeymoon. Mark and I had spent a lot of time apart.

I dropped my gaze to my plate. A part of me was still afraid that Mark would someday decide he'd made a mistake in marrying me. I couldn't stand to watch his expression when I told him why I suspected I felt guilty about the whole situation in case it made him start down that path. But I had to admit to it. I had to keep my vow to be honest with him. "Maybe it's because I feel like I put my work above my life."

Mark took my hand and tugged it gently toward him. It drew my gaze along with it.

He kissed my palm. "Our work is part of our lives. We're both in careers where we'll sometimes have to make choices about priorities that other people won't understand. The important thing is that we make those choices together whenever possible."

The way Mark said it left me unsure if he thought I'd done that or I hadn't. Or maybe that was my own insecurity showing through again because I wasn't sure. "Was that the case this time?"

"For the most part." Mark grinned. "Maybe not when you went running off in the middle of the night after two sentences of explanation."

I scooted my chair closer and leaned into him. "I think it was more than two."

"Fine." The smile in his voice let me know that he understood I was teasing rather than arguing. "Four, then."

That commitment to partnership was probably why my parents' marriage worked even though they spent long hours at work and didn't do a lot of the things that marriage experts would say people needed to do to have a great marriage. Everything they did was based on a choice they made together.

I felt bad for Carrie on more than one level. She'd likely married Garth in part because she wanted to be taken care of, but that also seemed to mean—if the authorities found him alive —she wouldn't have much of a say in their future. She wouldn't be an equal partner. I mean, what kind of man didn't even take his wife's preferences into account when choosing their honeymoon?

I straightened. A man who wasn't a good man.

What if the mistake I'd been making in all of this was assuming that Garth had to secretly be a good man because Carrie loved him?

Carrie didn't know him—not really. She'd only met him six weeks ago. If I removed the assumption that Garth must be a good man because Carrie loved and married him, then Carrie might well be a pawn in another of Garth's schemes.

A scheme that would have let him slip away to South America, the same way Robert Vesco had done, with all his embezzled money. With the investigation into Garth Bodie's activities ongoing, it would have looked suspicious for him to plan a trip out of the country—but not if he was going on his honeymoon, on a cruise with his new wife. He'd also have needed a way to make his disappearance less suspicious. The best way to do that was to stage a kidnapping or murder.

My chest tightened. Poor Carrie. If I was right, Garth sent that note telling her to get off the ship. He'd wanted to frame her for his disappearance, knowing his son would argue to anyone who would listen that Carrie had murdered his father for his money.

It even explained why his toiletries were gone from their room, but he'd left his wallet and passport behind. He'd planned to assume a new identity once he reached South America, but he'd needed his personal items to stay clean in the meantime. I'd made another unproven assumption when I thought Carrie grabbed his items by accident instead of her own.

It was the one scenario I hadn't considered. With the most likely suspects in Garth's disappearance crossed off the list, it left

us with the old Sherlock Holmes' saying. When you've eliminated the impossible, whatever remains, however improbable,
must be the truth.

Mark's fork clinked against his plate. "I don't like that look.
It's the look that says I'm not going to get to finish my breakfast."

If I was right, he might not. "I think I might have inadver-
tently made things worse."

Mark pushed back from the table slightly. "What things?"

I filled him in on my suspicion.

Mark pressed his fingers into the line above his eyebrows.
"Which means he'll have to find another way off the ship before
we get back to American soil."

I nodded. "And I think the only way for him to do that, short
of jumping into the Pacific Ocean, is to force everyone to
abandon ship."

We'd be picked up by South American rescue crews. He'd
have no trouble sneaking away once the rescue crews brought us
back to land.

Mark's skin had returned to its natural healthy color since
we'd found the source of his sickness. Now it took on a grey
tinge again. "People might panic, causing injuries, even accidental deaths."

A tiny part of me wanted to throw myself into his arms
because he had such trust in me and my instincts that, no matter
how crazy my ideas sounded, he believed me. The bigger, more

logical part of me knew we'd have plenty of time for falling into each other's arms later. Right now, we had to figure out how Garth Bodie planned to force an evacuation of a cruise ship in time to stop him.

CHAPTER 14

How did a man force a cruise ship full of over a thousand people to evacuate?

"We'd be forced to dock if there was a hurricane," Mark said, "but he can't manufacture one of those."

"Pirates?" The thought slipped out before I had time to stop it.

Mark raised an eyebrow at me. "Pirates?"

Okay, that one was crazy even for me. I'd heard of cruise ships having to stay away from certain routes to avoid pirates, but this wasn't one of those areas. Besides, it wasn't like Garth Bodie had pirate contacts hiding up his sleeve that he could call in on a whim.

That left only one thing I could think of. "Fire."

Mark's Adam's apple rode up in his throat and then plunged

down. "You can't trick the fire alarms on modern cruise ships with a cigarette or match. There are built-in heat sensors. He'd have to set an actual fire."

Dear Lord, no. An unnecessary evacuation was one thing, but a real fire was another. People could be trapped and burn to death. "How do we stop him?"

Mark glanced back toward the stage. I followed his gaze. The captain was still there, answering questions from a group of passengers who'd clustered around him.

"I'll talk to him," Mark said.

He didn't say so, but he didn't have to—the captain was more likely to respond to a request from Mark. It'd been clear the captain hadn't liked the way I'd forced him into doing what I wanted last night. As much as I hated being outside the loop, Mark was right, and letting him do this was part of working as a team.

Five minutes passed with me squirming in my seat as Mark tried to get the captain alone to speak to him. He couldn't explain what we thought was going on with passengers around. Panic would have roared through the ship faster than a fire.

It was like watching an old silent movie, their hand gestures and facial expressions telling me as much as words could have. Even in jeans and a t-shirt, Mark managed to look professional. We'd often talked about how he had trouble in social situations, but when he was working, no one handled themselves as well as he did—in my biased opinion, anyway.

The captain's body language closed down, and he shook his head. Mark said something more. The captain crossed his arms.

Mark turned around and walked back toward me. I rose to my feet. The captain wasn't going to listen. He thought we were making trouble for our own benefit now. Or something like that. Whatever reason he gave Mark didn't matter. I could tell even from this distance that he wasn't going to act on our suspicions.

Which meant we had to figure something out ourselves. And fast.

Mark took my hand as if we were just going to leave the dining hall and return to whatever we'd originally planned for the day.

"We're going up top, near the lifeboats," Mark said quietly. "If this goes wrong before we can figure out a way to stop it, I don't want you trampled."

"Maybe it'll be more like the *Titanic* and people won't take it seriously enough to panic."

I scrunched up my nose. That wasn't my best analogy. A lot of people died on the *Titanic* who didn't have to *because* they didn't take the need to evacuate seriously. I certainly didn't want a repeat of that here.

Mark, graciously, didn't respond.

We didn't know where to start looking, and we were only two people. Even if Mark would agree to running around the ship separately right now—which his insistence on heading for the lifeboats made a slim possibility—the odds of us finding Garth Bodie before he set a fire weren't great.

We needed help.

The problem was that the people most likely to be able to find Garth and stop him were the security personnel, and they'd all want to check with the captain before helping us. If he hadn't been willing to mobilize them after Mark spoke to him, he wasn't going to change his mind after we tried to go behind his back.

The only way to circumvent the captain seemed to be to enlist the help of someone the security officers would obey without going to the captain first. Someone who would believe us quickly that Garth Bodie was capable of doing something like this and who would want to stop him from escaping.

I tugged on Mark's hand. "We need to find out where they're holding Hart."

THE FEMALE OFFICER WHO'D LOOKED AT ME SUSPICIOUSLY BEFORE was the one in the security office when we arrived. It took claiming to be Hart's legal counsel and a phone call back to my partner Anderson in Michigan to convince her to take us to him. The captain had posted two other security personnel outside his quarters.

Hart tapped a staccato beat on his thighs as I explained to him what we thought happened and what we needed from him. "This isn't some trick?"

There didn't seem to be anything I could gain from trying to trick him except to get his staff into trouble. I couldn't think of a single reason I'd want to do that. "No trick. Remember how I said I'm after the truth?"

He nodded.

"I'm still after it, and I don't want to see you convicted of a crime you didn't commit."

Hart rocked back in his chair.

We didn't have time to wait for him to make his decision. My parents were either going to be very annoyed or very proud of me for my next bargaining tactic. "If you help with this and we're able to catch Bodie, I'll make sure you're represented by the top criminal defense firm in the country for a price you can afford."

Since he'd basically confessed, he might not be acquitted, but my parents' firm could at least bargain for a lenient sentence.

"Call my staff in," Hart said.

Watching him talk to his people made me even more glad that I'd offered to get him represented by my parents' firm. Only one of the three security officers present stopped to confirm that he wouldn't try to leave the room while they were gone. And they all took Hart at his word when he said he'd stay put.

The female officer left him with her radio, saying she'd get another one from storage while they called in the off-duty officers. Hart would need the radio to coordinate their search, she said.

We stayed with Hart and listened to them talk back and forth as they searched the most likely spots for Garth to start a fire. Hart had figured them out based on the fact that he believed Garth would want the best chance at making it safely off the ship himself once he started things rolling.

About a half an hour into their search, one of the teams went silent. At least I thought they did. The chatter seemed to lessen. I grabbed Mark's arm.

"We got him," a man's voice crackled through the radio. "But I sure hope they'll call the Coast Guard this time. Based on the fight he put up, I don't think he's going to stay quietly in his room like you are, Rick."

Hart got up and headed for the phone, presumably to call the captain himself.

With Hart's back turned to us, Mark leaned down and gave me a kiss that sent heat shooting straight through my body.

"When the captain hears he has to call the Coast Guard," Mark whispered, "I think he'll find a way to make sure we don't get our voucher for another trip."

"That's okay." I leaned in. "For our next honeymoon, I'd much rather go someplace where there aren't any other people.

That way, we can be sure we won't be interrupted by another crime."

Mark laughed, and I cut it off it with a kiss full of the promise of many more to come.

GINGER DEAD MAN

A CUPCAKE TRUCK NOVELLA

The two homeless people staring at my food truck from across the street made my skin break out into a clammy sweat.

I loosened my scarf and handed my lone customer her cupcake and coffee. December in Michigan, as it turned out, wasn't a very profitable time to be a food truck. No one walked anywhere, let alone wanted to stand in a line while the wind cut them to tatters. I'd sold five cupcakes all day.

My customer left, and the only people remaining on the street were me and the homeless man and woman across the road from me. Maybe it was time to close up and move on.

I climbed out of my truck and unlatched the first support bar that held my front flap open.

It wasn't that I had anything against homeless people. In fact, I stopped each morning to give a coffee and a cupcake to an older man busking on the street in the snow. It wasn't much, but it was what I had to offer. My margins were so tight right now that I was only eating once a day myself.

The man looked so vulnerable, with his scraggly white beard and coat two sizes too big, that when he asked me to stay and visit with him while he ate, I always did. In return, he gave me tips about the best places to park my truck to try to find more business—or, at least, the places he'd had the most luck begging for money. Yesterday, he pulled up his pant leg to show me the new socks he'd bought—bright orange with green stripes—to prove to me that he was trying to get money for things he really needed.

His name was Jimmy, he'd said. And he'd made a lot of mistakes. He'd ended up on the streets because he drank his life away.

And that last part was what worried me about the two homeless people now whispering to each other across the street from where I parked.

Many in the homeless community could be bribed with alcohol, drugs, or money. They were the kind of people my husband could easily convince to help him find me. If Jarrod found me, I'd be dead.

The homeless pair crossed the street, the woman in the lead.

My fingers went cold despite the sweat still beading on my upper lip. Maybe they were simply going to ask me for money or some food. Logically, I knew that was the most likely reason for them to approach me.

But Fear screamed at me that they'd been sent by Jarrod. And I trusted Fear. He kept me safe.

My deadened fingers made it hard for me to release the last clasp. It took me two tries. I finally lowered the flap and secured it into place.

"Hey," a woman's voice said from much too close behind me.

I turned around slowly, even though my heart beat as if I'd been sprinting down the street.

The woman stood close enough to make me uncomfortable, but not close enough that I could really say she was inside my personal bubble. Her eyes were bloodshot, and the broken capillaries around her nose suggested she was a drinker. Her breath backed that guess up.

The man now stood next to her. He was shorter than her by a couple inches, but broader. He wore his long blond hair pulled back in a ponytail.

"Sorry." I shuffled a step to the side in the direction of my door. "I'm closed."

"We're not here for food," the man said.

"I'd take something for free," the woman grumbled under her breath.

I slid sideways another few inches and fished around in my pocket for my keys. The woman sounded like she might be happy to get a handout and leave, but the man's words were almost threatening. If they weren't there for food, there was only one other reason I could think of for them to be there. They were trying to figure out if I might be the woman they'd been hired to find.

Except his tone of voice wasn't threatening. It sounded almost humble.

The part of me that had insisted I stop to feed Jimmy wanted to give them both cupcakes and a cup of hot cocoa. It wasn't like I was going to sell all the cupcakes anyway. And they were delicious. I was working on perfecting a gingerbread cupcake with eggnog icing. Jimmy raved about my latest tweak to the recipe.

If you feed them, Fear whispered, *maybe you can buy their loyalty.*

I doubted that. Jarrod had a lot more to offer than I did, but it was worth a shot to distract them at least.

I edged toward my truck door until the handle hit my back. "I could get you a couple cupcakes if you'd like. I don't serve anything else except coffee."

My voice sounded a lot calmer than I felt.

"No," the man said at the same time as the woman said, "Yeah."

They exchanged a look. Hers clearly said *why not?* while his said *stick with the plan.*

She crossed her arms over her chest. "Jimmy said they were good."

The tightness in my chest eased. Maybe I was letting my past drive my present too much. If they were here because I'd been kind to Jimmy, then I didn't want to seem mean to them by leaving. Not only did I always hear my dad in my head telling me to show mercy to those who needed it most, but showing kindness to them would hopefully make them allies and not enemies in case I needed allies in the future.

"It's no problem if you'd like one." I forced out a smile and concentrated on making it big enough to crinkle my eyes. It was a trick I'd figured out. Fake smiles didn't normally reach the eyes. "I think they're good, too, but I'm biased."

The man held out a hand in front of the woman as if to stop her from accepting my offer. "Maybe after. We need your help first."

It's a trick, Fear said. *Run.*

But they had me curious now. What help could I possibly offer other than to give them food or money? I didn't have any money to give, and they'd already turned down my food...or at least the man had.

"I'm Dwayne," the man said. "This is Carla. We're friends of Jimmy, and we haven't seen him in over a day."

Living on the streets, my assumption would be they often didn't see each other every day. Perhaps the opposite was true. Perhaps they watched out for each other more than they would have if they'd had their own apartments, jobs, and regular lives.

Perhaps I was the only one who didn't have someone watching out for me.

Dwayne's introduction still didn't tell me why they'd sought me out. It did ease my mind that they hadn't been sent by Jarrod. He would have had to be watching me for a while to know about Jimmy. If he knew my location for that long, I'd have already been dead and buried.

"What brings you to me?" I asked. The question sounded strangely formal, but I wanted to find the right balance between sorting this out so I could get out of the cold and being polite.

"We need a ride to find him." Carla scrubbed her running nose on her sleeve. "We don't have money for a cab."

Her voice sounded annoyed that Jimmy would cause her this much trouble. It wasn't the same worried vibe I got from Dwayne.

The fleeting thought about how I'd be safer if I had the favor of those in the homeless community came back to me.

And it wasn't like I'd be losing any business. I'd been sitting here for three hours now, and the lunch time "rush" of the handful of people who'd braved the cold was long past.

Silly as it sounded, my conversations with Jimmy had been the high points of my week. Most people would only see how I'd been kind to him, but he'd also been kind to me. For a little bit, sitting on the street and eating cupcakes with a homeless man, I'd felt normal.

"Do you know where he would be?" As much as I wanted to help, I wasn't going to spend my whole day driving every back street in the city. I couldn't even if I wanted to. It would burn too much gas.

Dwayne pursed his lips. "Jimmy hunts in the dumpsters for stuff he can fix up and sell."

"He should know better," Carla interjected, not quite under her breath.

Dwayne didn't even glance her way, as if he wanted to pretend he hadn't heard her. I decided to follow his lead.

"We're worried he fell climbing in and out and might be lying hurt somewhere," he said. "He's not as young as he used to be."

Dwayne's skin was so weathered that I couldn't guess at his exact age, but I would have probably put Jimmy in his fifties. Definitely not old, but perhaps that was considered elderly when you lived on the streets.

Carla looked to be somewhere in between Dwayne and Jimmy in age, though her behavior at least was much less mature than either. It grated on me. I couldn't peg exactly why, but I had a suspicion it was because she was a woman and I was a woman, and I didn't like anyone giving my gender a bad reputation.

"Do you know his regular spots?" I asked.

"Every single one," Dwayne said. "I helped him find the ones where people were most likely to throw the good stuff."

That anything in a dumpster could be considered *good stuff* baffled me. Dumpsters had always given me the creeps. I imagined them full of rotting meat and maggots.

Then again, I'd read an article in The Positivity Project column from a town not far from here that talked about people who lived off of discarded food. They didn't do it because they couldn't afford it. Most of them had regular jobs. They did it from the moral standpoint of wanting to reduce the unnecessary waste North Americans were famous for.

Though, if business didn't pick up, I might be eating from dumpsters for an entirely different reason.

Or I'd be joining Jimmy, Dwayne, and Carla at whatever shelter or mission in the city provided hot meals.

I motioned for Dwayne and Carla to climb into the cab of my truck. I'd barely pulled out onto the road before Carla was complaining about how the seatbelt was uncomfortable and how I needed to turn up the heat because not everyone had nice socks like I did.

I wasn't sure how she knew from a glance that my socks were any better than hers—one of mine actually had a hole in the toe—but it seemed like homeless people had a bit of an obsession with socks.

I drove them from alleyway to alleyway, with Dwayne hopping out at every stop. Carla used her less convenient seat as an excuse to stay inside the cab with me. All the stops blurred together except for the one where Dwayne found a homeless man sleeping under a cardboard blanket and another dumpster that Dwayne said smelled so rancid he'd been afraid he might find Jimmy—or someone else—dead inside.

After almost two hours, it'd started to snow, and the snowflakes melted as soon as Dwayne entered the overly-warm cab, leaving him looking like he'd been dunked in a bucket of water.

"That's the last one," he said.

His tone made my heart feel like someone had stepped on it. No matter who you were, losing a friend or family member was hard. I could only imagine not knowing what happened to them was even worse. I'd only known Jimmy a few days, and worry for him was going to make it hard for me to sleep tonight.

Carla snuffled again. The warm truck seemed to have only made her runny nose worse. "There's one more spot. At the train tracks."

"He never went there with me." Dwayne snapped his seatbelt back in, as if he expected me to follow her directions. "There's nothing good there."

"He don't tell you everything. Some things we kept between him and me." There was a proprietary feel to Carla's words, like she had a different connection with Jimmy than Dwayne did.

I asked for directions and put my truck into drive. We passed a mission on the way, and Dwayne pointed it out to me as the one where they usually slept. Even though it wasn't yet four o'clock, people already lined up down the streets.

"We probably won't get a bed tonight thanks to Jimmy," Carla said.

And for not the first time, I wondered if it was even possible to get into her good graces. At least I'd have hopefully earned a bit of loyalty from Dwayne—and Jimmy, if we ever found him.

The train station was back a few streets from the mission, but still an easy walk.

I parked along the side of the chain-link fence that Carla pointed toward.

This time, instead of staying in the truck, she got out. It was a good thing she did. Since Dwayne didn't know Jimmy's spots on the railroad property, it'd have taken him until well past dark to search all the possible locations Jimmy might be.

Her feet hit the ground, and she turned back toward me. "Ain't you coming?"

I hadn't planned to. They'd seemed happy with my role of chauffeur before now.

Dwayne leaned around Carla. "We could use the extra hands. It's a lot further to carry him out from here."

Of course. That made sense. They had no intention of calling for help even if he was hurt. Ambulances and hospitals cost money—money none of us had.

I turned the truck off, locked it, and followed Carla to a break in the fence.

The irony that the hole was right next to a *No Trespassing* sign wasn't lost on me. I opened my mouth to point it out to Carla and Dwayne, but they'd already ducked through the hole. Undoubtedly it wasn't the first *No Trespassing* sign they'd ignored.

We picked our way over tracks that were clearly inactive based on the amount of accumulated rust. Closer to the front of the yard, a passenger train pulled to a stop in front of the station, and off in the distance, another train whistle sounded.

"What did he pick here?" Dwayne asked over his shoulder to Carla. "Ain't nobody whose gonna buy steel from one of us. They'd know it was stolen."

Carla's gaze shifted to the side. "I didn't say he picked stuff here. I said it was one of our spots. The empty cars are a good place for drinking and other stuff we can't do at the mission."

The gap before she answered made me think she was lying, but I had no proof and no reason for why she would.

Except all the abandoned cars we passed seemed to have padlocks on the doors.

A shiver went down my spine and left me feeling colder than the snow down my collar had.

This had been a stupid idea. Helping out a few homeless people wasn't going to stop all the others from aiding Jarrod if he figured out where I was. And it seemed less likely all the time that we'd find Jimmy.

Assuming he was missing in the first place. For all I knew, this was all a ploy to lure me out here and rob me.

We moved on to a section of the railyard with tracks that seemed well-kept and used.

Carla passed the edge of the next train car and disappeared from sight. Two steps later, Dwayne turned the corner as well.

I hung back. Maybe I should turn around now and leave them here. They weren't that far from the mission. They could walk back.

No one could blame me for cutting my losses. The sun was already dipping in the sky, and I still needed to find a safe place to park my truck for the night.

Carla and Dwayne weren't the only ones who were homeless.

I backed up a step.

A female screech and a string of loud curse words from a male voice burst from behind the train car.

I froze. That couldn't be good.

Instead of continuing on my path back to my truck, I jogged forward. I couldn't leave them now. I didn't know if either of them had a cell phone to call for help if they needed it.

I peeked around the corner just to be sure there wasn't a fight going on. If there was, I'd call the police to come break it up and then make my retreat before they got here.

There wasn't a fight.

Instead, Carla and Dwayne stood on either side of a mangled body draped across the train tracks.

CHAPTER 2

The first thing I noticed about the dead man was his bare feet.

At least, I assumed it was a man, based on his feet. They seemed to be too large, with too much hair on the toes, for a woman.

A pair of scuffed boots lay next to the tracks, their laces untied, like the man had taken them off before lying down along the tracks. A nearly empty case of beer rested nearby, and the air reeked of hops.

I didn't move any closer. I didn't need a better look at the rest of the man to know he was dead.

Bile burned the back of my throat. The sound of Dwayne losing whatever he'd eaten for lunch came from my right, and I clamped a hand over my mouth.

Shows like *CSI* flashed images of butchered bodies and

autopsies all the time. I just had to pretend this was a TV show, too. That body was all painted plastic and CGI effects. It wasn't real.

Tricking my brain worked enough that I could lower my hand. My stomach still felt a bit like I was riding a rollercoaster, though. I'd only ridden a rollercoaster once, and I'd never been a fan of it. It didn't make sense to me any more than watching horror movies did. I was scared enough of things in life that were real. I didn't need to manufacture fear for the "fun" of it.

Carla had moved away from the body. She now sat on the steps leading up into an empty car, staring off into nothing.

Dwayne straightened.

Presumably, they saw a lot of sickening things on the streets. His reaction seemed strong.

I had a bad feeling I knew why. "Is it Jimmy?"

Dwayne nudged the beer case with his toe. "I don't get it."

I didn't get it, either. I was no psychiatrist, but Jimmy hadn't seemed suicidal to me. He'd seemed accepting of his past failures in a way that made me think he was focused on improvement, not on punishing himself.

And yet, he'd taken off his shoes. Why would someone do that in the middle of winter, when it was cold enough out to get frostbite if you weren't careful?

Maybe he was so drunk he didn't know what he was doing.

My mind had the grinding feeling it got when it wanted to make sense of something senseless. I'd be up all night turning this over in my brain, trying to figure it out and asking why it'd happened.

But I'd have time for that later. Right now, I had to deal with what was in front of me.

I backed in the direction of the train car I'd come around when I heard them find Jimmy. "You need to call the police."

Carla shook her head. It was the first movement I'd seen her make. "We can't call the police. They'll think we killed him."

I doubted that. There weren't any trains traveling this set of tracks at the moment, but they did run as far as I could see in either direction, and they seemed to arc to meet up with the main line. Clearly Jimmy had somehow laid down on the tracks, and the conductor didn't see him.

It was strange, though, that they hadn't felt it when they hit him. Maybe they'd simply thought it was non-living debris on the tracks?

Regardless, I couldn't call the police. The police would want my name. I couldn't give them my name.

I held up my hands. Hopefully they'd think I'd forgotten my phone in my truck even though it was safely stashed in my pocket. "Does one of you have a phone? It'll be nearly impossible for you to explain why I'm here, and you can be each other's alibi."

Carla gave me a look that said I clearly didn't know what I was talking about.

"We could leave him here." The pallor to Dwayne's skin

suggested he was struggling to keep from throwing up again. "There's nothing the police or anyone can do for him now."

Carla hopped down from the steps. "We can't leave him here like he's trash. He deserves a burial."

Her voice reminded me of a child who'd been repeatedly bullied when they were talking about something they were good at.

And for a second, I understood Carla better than almost anyone else probably could.

She couldn't stand leaving Jimmy there to rot until someone else found him. Doing so treated him like he was worthless simply because he'd been homeless rather than as a human being who deserved respect. If she allowed that, she'd be saying she wasn't worth anything more than being left for rats and other scavengers to eat once she died.

She probably wouldn't have been able to articulate all that even if I asked her, but I heard it in her voice nonetheless. I heard it because I knew what it was like to be told you were worthless enough times that you started to believe it.

Homeless people weren't often told it, but they felt it in the way people treated them and looked at them.

I understood, but I wasn't a knight in shining armor. I could barely take care of myself.

"Do either of you have a cell phone?" I asked again.

Dwayne patted his pocket. "I do." His skin turned even more pasty. "It's one Jimmy found and fixed up for me."

I felt sick for an entirely different reason. There was no such thing as fair in this world. It seemed like the good people suffered while people like Jarrod could do whatever they wanted.

I wasn't sure what camp I fell in. I knew what it was to suffer, but I wouldn't have called myself a good person. Especially given what I had to do next.

I nodded at Dwayne. "Then you two will have to decide what to do. I can't stay."

I backed up until I rounded the corner of the train car, and then took off at a jog.

Carla's curses chased after me.

Even though I'd helped them find Jimmy, I certainly hadn't earned any favors in return. In fact, if Jarrod ever came looking for me, I had an uncomfortable feeling that Carla would offer to help him find me without asking for anything in return.

CHAPTER 3

I'd thought I was as hypervigilant as a person could get. I'd
been wrong.

For the next week, I closed up my truck and moved
every time I saw someone who might be homeless. The names
Carla called me as I left, and the threats that went along with
those names, left me feeling like she might one day sneak up
behind me and hit me in the head with an iron pipe.

I couldn't have explained why I thought it would be an iron
pipe. Logically, those were probably in as short supply as
wrenches and hammers on the street. She more likely would
have stabbed me with a homemade shiv. But in my nightmares,
it was always a pipe.

And sometimes she looked like Jarrod.

So when I opened my front flap and Dwayne and Carla stood

not five feet from my truck, my first thought was that I was dreaming.

My second was that at least she'd probably kill me quicker than Jarrod would.

I must have caught them by surprise by opening the door because we stared at each other for almost thirty seconds without saying anything.

Dwayne reached out a hand toward me as if he realized I was considering closing the door in their faces. "We need your help again."

Carla didn't make eye contact with me. "And those cupcakes you offered last time."

Yeah, inviting them inside sounded like a great idea. They could beat me up without risking witnesses then.

Fear stayed quiet in my head, probably because he didn't need to say anything. I was frightened enough already without his input.

Dwayne gave Carla a look that said *keep going*.

She huffed out a breath. "I'm sorry for yelling last time. I have a temper, and I was upset about Jimmy."

As grudging as her apology sounded, it also sounded sincere. And there was a tremor to her hands that suggested she was either detoxing or really hungry.

I couldn't turn them away if it was the latter. Besides, if I fed her, I wouldn't need to keep watch for her as well as Jarrod from this point forward.

I stepped back to give them room to enter. "It's a tight fit. You'll need to sit on the floor."

"We're used to sitting on the ground," Dwayne said. "We don't mind the floor."

Point taken.

I got them both a hot cup of coffee and a gingerbread cupcake. With Christmas less than a week away, the gingerbread cupcakes were selling, and a couple of people who'd tried them had spread the word enough that I even got asked to provide desserts for a couple of last-minute office Christmas parties. It was going to be enough to keep me going for a little longer.

Dwayne polished off his cupcake before saying anything, as if he were afraid it might disappear if he didn't take advantage of it. He reminded me a bit of a stray puppy being offered a meal of scraps.

"Here's the thing." He paused and licked his fingers—which made me shudder. "We called the police like you told us to, but they're saying Jimmy's death was an accident. They say he got drunk, passed out, and the train hit him. The driver probably thought he hit a chunk of ice or something."

I poured myself a mug of coffee even though I didn't want to drink another cup. It was something warm to wrap my hands around.

An accidental death sounded possible to me. I'd wondered about it, too, except for the shoes. No one removes their shoes in winter before accidentally passing out.

But I wanted to hear what made Dwayne and Carla think it wasn't an accident. "Go on."

"The police are wrong," Carla said.

Stating that something was the truth didn't make it so. If they wanted me or the police or anyone to believe them, they needed more than that. They needed evidence. "Why do you think the police are wrong? Did Jimmy never drink or something?"

I knew he had. He'd told me so himself. What I wanted to see was whether Carla would admit it or lie to me. That would help me figure out if the rest of what they were going to say was the truth or not.

Carla scooched over and, without asking, took another cupcake from the plate I'd brought out of the fridge. "Oh, he drank alright."

Dwayne looked at her as if he was considering slapping her hand but knew it wouldn't do anything other than make her angry. "He drank, but never beer. Jimmy hated beer. Wouldn't touch it even if it was free."

The alcohol next to his body had definitely been a case of beer. That, along with the weird shoe situation, made me think they could be right. "Did you tell the police that?"

Dwayne nodded. "They didn't seem to believe us."

No, they probably wouldn't have. In their eyes, Jimmy was a drunk, and it'd sound crazy to say a drunk wouldn't drink anything alcoholic presented to them.

When I talked to him, Jimmy had sounded truly regretful for all the things heavy drinking had cost him, too. Granted, I hadn't known him long, but I couldn't see him getting fall-down drunk on a drink he didn't even like.

I sipped my coffee to buy myself time to answer.

I wasn't going to try to convince the police if that's what they were after in terms of help. In fact, now that this was a police matter, I needed to be as far away from the situation as possible. "I didn't know Jimmy well enough to change the investigating officer's mind."

"They don't need to know that," Carla said. "Just tell 'em you're a friend of his family or something."

Lie to the police, in other words. Not happening. "I've really got to get going. I have a catering event to bake for."

Dwayne jumped to his feet from a sitting position faster than anyone should have been able to. "We can trade information for help. We know the best spots for you to park for the night where no one will bother you."

My hands lost their grip on my mug. I grabbed it again just in time to avoid singeing my lap.

They knew I was living in my truck. That wasn't good. At all. While it wasn't technically illegal to sleep in your vehicle in Michigan, it broke a lot of health and safety laws for a food truck.

Dwayne's offer sounded genuine, like he simply thought he was offering something I'd want—and he was. Right now, I was using my cell phone to check for infrared security cameras. When it was dark out, if I didn't see a light with my naked eye, but I did see a light when looking at the same spot through my phone's camera screen, I knew there was a security camera. That didn't tell me about security patrols and how busy an area was, though. It only made sure I wouldn't be caught on camera. I could use a more reliable source for safe spots to park for the night.

Besides, if I turned them away without any help, Carla might get angry again and figure out she could use my living situation against me.

Despite that, I couldn't go to the police. I wouldn't go to the police. I also didn't want to lose my catering gigs by leaving town. I was already getting dizzy spells from how little I ate.

So I had to figure out what I could do to aid them without putting myself into the line of sight of the police.

I did know someone who might be able to look into it and make sure the police were doing their due diligence in investigating it. Assuming she was home from her honeymoon.

I hadn't planned to call Nicole Fitzhenry-Dawes, the last catering client I'd had in Fair Haven before I'd had to move on. I didn't want to leave a trail between her and me for Jarrod to follow.

But she did have connections.

I stood up and set my cup on the counter. "I don't want to lie to the police, but I know someone who might be able to find out if there was alcohol in Jimmy's bloodstream or if he had any defensive wounds. Would that be good enough?"

Dwayne and Carla exchanged a glance that I couldn't read.

"That's fair," Dwayne said. "If it looks like he drank it himself, we'll tell you the spots and let it be."

I cared about the spots a lot less than I cared about avoiding Carla's retribution, but I decided it was better to let him think we were making a "business" deal.

Now I just had to hope Nicole was home and that she really could help.

When my call went straight to voicemail, I assumed Nicole was still on her honeymoon. So that I would have a ready excuse for Dwayne and Carla, I left a message anyway with what I needed.

Nicole's name showed up on my cell phone a day later as I was removing the last batch of cupcakes from the oven for the party I was catering that night.

I turned the oven off and answered the call.

"I'm glad you called," Nicole said. "Are you okay?"

She was the only person in Michigan who knew the truth about me. I'd refused to tell her where I was going when I'd left Fair Haven, and not only because I wasn't sure myself. I hadn't wanted to put her at risk of Jarrod using her to get to me.

Now that she knew what county I was in, I should relocate—as soon as the holidays were over and my catering jobs had padded my bank account enough to make sure my truck had enough gas to leave the county at all.

I filled Nicole in on everything that'd gone on since I moved on from Fair Haven, leaving out keys bits about how I'd been skipping a lot of meals. I ended with the newest development.

"I thought you were playing a joke on me," Nicole said, "until Mark found there was a homeless man named James Turner hit by a train in Redmond."

"I wish it was a joke. How was your honeymoon?"

I cringed as soon as the words were out of my mouth. That always seemed like one of those questions where there was nothing but awkward answers. If the person answered too enthusiastically, they opened themselves up for winks and nudges. If they answered too mildly, people would speculate on the state of their new marriage.

Nicole laughed. "That's a story in itself. Once we deal with your potential crime, I'll tell you about mine. For now, let's just say we have a voucher for another cruise in the future."

If I'd been talking to anyone else, I would have thought they were joking. One thing I'd discovered about Nicole in our short acquaintance, though, was she had an uncanny knack for ending up involved in murder cases, and not only because she was a criminal defense attorney.

The sound of ruffling paper filtered through from her end. It made me think she was looking for the piece of paper where she'd taken some notes for me. "Mark's helped the medical examiner for your county out a couple of times, so he called in a favor to see the report. There was too much damage to the body for the medical examiner to tell if there were defensive wounds. He did check even though the police wanted to call it an accident. But there were two things that didn't match up."

Presumably Nicole meant two things other than the beer and the removed shoes. I hadn't told her about any of that. Which meant that we were up to four things that didn't fit with how the police wanted to explain away the situation.

I wasn't like Nicole. I didn't think the police cared about everyone and all cases equally. At least, not police outside of Fair Haven. "I bet I can guess the first one. He didn't have any alcohol in his bloodstream."

"None. Not even as much as you'd get from drinking mouthwash."

People did that? Yuck. "What's the other thing?"

"Some of his wounds were post-mortem. Mark thinks he was already dead when the train hit him."

I sank down to the floor and leaned back against my cupboards. That also meant someone had beaten him to death prior to laying him on the train tracks.

It was what I'd always been afraid of every time Jarrod beat me. I used to wonder what would happen if one day he went too far and accidentally killed me. How would he have hidden my body?

"So I guess I have good news and bad news," Nicole said,

drawing my attention back to the present. "The good news is that the medical examiner is going to insist the police reopen the case as a murder. The bad news is that James Turner was murdered."

I THOUGHT I'D NEVER SEE DWAYNE AND CARLA AGAIN AFTER I told them that the police were reopening Jimmy's case as a murder investigation.

A few days before Christmas, they found me again. I leaned out the front flap of my truck to see if any more potential customers were headed my way, and instead spotted them crossing the street.

Carla walked in a way that made me think she was stomping her feet.

I stayed at the window and kept my door closed. Whatever trouble they were dragging in their wake this time, they were going to have to go somewhere else.

Carla arrived first and examined my chalkboard menu as if she were going to place an order—except I knew if she did, no money would exchange hands for it.

Dwayne caught up before Carla could make her decision.

I propped my arms up on the counter. Maybe they were simply here to give me an update and not to drag me off into another problem.

I'd checked the newspaper every day, but there hadn't been even a mention of Jimmy's death. "Any updates on the case?"

Dwayne nodded and rubbed his hands together. The gloves he wore were missing a finger. "Can we come inside where it's warmer?"

Don't you dare, Fear said in my head. *Don't you let them in. They're nothing but trouble.*

He was probably right, but Carla gave me a look that said she'd have no trouble popping someone in the nose who wouldn't take pity on two freezing homeless people. Truth be told, I was still more afraid of her than I was of whatever they might try to drag me in to.

I bit back a sigh and pulled my sign in out of the window. "Drop my flap for me. It'll keep the heat in for us."

They did, and then entered without waiting for another invite.

Carla went straight for my fridge and fished out the pumpkin cupcake I'd recently developed to go along with my Christmas catering gigs.

Carla scarfed the cupcake down in two bites. "They don't care nothing about the death of a homeless man."

They had to refer to the police. Which put me in a difficult spot. I wanted to argue that I was sure they were doing everything they could—that answer was the most likely to get Carla out of my truck before she ate up my profits.

But I wasn't sure, and they might realize I was simply trying to placate them.

Instead I opted for another question. "What makes you say that?"

"'Cause it's true."

She moved toward the fridge again. I stepped in front of her as if I were reaching for the coffee pot. I hadn't planned to offer them anything, but Dwayne was still shivering. Hopefully he wasn't coming down with anything. "Let me rephrase. Why do you think that?"

I gave them both a cup of coffee, and I motioned Dwayne to my folding chair. It didn't seem right expecting him to sit on the floor.

Dwayne sank into my chair, and I sat in front of the fridge. I felt a little selfish not letting Carla continue to forage, but I had to set boundaries somewhere. If she asked, I'd give her another. I wouldn't continue to let her take whatever she wanted.

Jarrod had always gotten whatever he wanted, bullying me with his temper tantrums and fists. One thing I'd promised myself when I got this truck was that it'd be mine and that no one would take it from me. Generosity wasn't generosity if it was forced from you.

"We went to the police to find out if they had any leads or anything." There was a rattle to Dwayne's voice that hadn't been there before. "Carla and Jimmy was married, so they have to tell her at least that much, we figured."

My gaze snapped to Carla before I could stop it. More questions ran through my head than I could put words to. Like what Jimmy saw in her. And whether they'd ended up on the street together or had met afterward.

I was smart enough not to ask any of them. "What did they tell you?"

"He said they couldn't discuss an active case with us, and that we needed to not come by anymore and take up police time."

Dwayne drank the last of his coffee in a chugging motion that probably scalded his throat. I refilled the mug for him.

The officer they'd spoken to had been rude, yes. That didn't mean they weren't actively investigating Jimmy's murder.

"Thing is, though," Dwayne said, "he didn't know what case we was talking about until we told him it was the guy who got hit by a train."

"And then he got Jimmy's name wrong," Carla added. "Twice. Even after I corrected him."

I cringed. There was no explaining that away. "He was the officer assigned to the case?"

Dwayne and Carla nodded in unison like they'd practiced it.

"They're never gonna find who killed him," Carla said. "'Cause the death of a homeless man don't matter."

My throat suddenly felt blocked. Swallowing didn't help.

Jarrod's words echoed in my mind about how no one would believe me if I reported him. No one would take my word over his. Because he was an important man, and I was nothing.

I didn't matter.

I'd stayed long past when I should have left and paid a cost much too high—all because I'd believed him.

Dwayne sipped his coffee more slowly this time. "We were thinking that maybe you'd be willing to help us find whoever killed him. You have connections and stuff."

He had to mean Nicole. I wasn't going to pull Nicole into this. She couldn't be anywhere near me.

Carla reached around me and grabbed the handle to my fridge. She pulled the door open, forcing me to move aside. She closed the door, another cupcake in her hand. "Besides, you can talk to people we can't. They don't know you're one of us."

She met my gaze and shoved the whole cupcake into her mouth.

I couldn't help but feel her words were a threat. *They don't know you're one of us, but we could tell them. No one will want to buy cupcakes from a woman living in her truck. The health department will shut you down, and then you won't think you're too good to help us.*

I wouldn't put it past her to do it. What she didn't know was that I could pack up after this week and vanish to another town where she'd have no way to carry out her threat.

But I couldn't escape myself.

When I'd been in Fair Haven, I'd helped Nicole solve a different murder. I hadn't wanted to. I'd wanted to stay as far away from the police as possible. But she'd reminded me that even though I hadn't been able to bring Jarrod to justice for what he did to me, I might have other chances to protect other people from bad cops.

I held out my hand to Dwayne for a handshake, my small way of letting Carla know I was doing this because I felt it was the right thing to do and not because she'd threatened me. "I'll do my best to help you figure out who murdered Jimmy."

CHAPTER 5

The first question we needed to answer was one of motive.

Hopefully it was a motive that would point specifically to someone. The unfortunate truth about life on the streets was that the homeless were vulnerable. Jimmy could have been killed by another homeless person who thought he'd taken their spot or their jacket or looked at them the wrong way—especially if the murderer was high at the time.

If that were the situation, our chances of figuring out who was responsible were slimmer than the chances of me running around in a bathing suit during a Michigan winter.

"Did anyone have a problem with Jimmy?" I didn't explicitly state *anyone in the homeless community*. Carla probably wouldn't have reacted well if I did.

Dwayne looked perkier with every cup of coffee I poured

into him. "Not one of us. Jimmy was careful not to take anyone's spot, and everyone liked him 'cause he shared what he found."

"He didn't always share." Carla's voice turned grumpy again. "Sometimes he kept it for himself."

Dwayne scowled at her. "Sometimes you keep stuff for yourself, too."

I got the impression that Jimmy and Carla's marriage hadn't been a happy one. It made me wonder who Dwayne was. He didn't look enough like either of them to be their son, and I didn't see enough affection between him and Carla for him to be her lover. In fact, they barely seemed to like each other. The only thing that brought them together appeared to be Jimmy.

And they both believed that he'd been murdered and also that no one had a motive to murder him. That wouldn't make his killer easy to find.

One valuable thing I'd taken away from being married to an FBI agent was that sometimes you had to ask potential suspects the same thing in different ways before you got the truth.

"What about arguments? Did Jimmy recently disagree with anyone?"

Dwayne glanced at Carla. For a second, I thought he was going to tell me that she was the one Jimmy fought with the most.

That was probably me projecting my dislike for Carla onto him.

He brought his coffee mug to his lips and then pulled it away, squinting inside as if caught off guard that the coffee was gone. "He had a loud argument with the manager of the mission where we usually stay. She doesn't usually argue with no one. He was so angry he refused to go back."

"He was selfish." Carla eyed my fridge but didn't make a move for it again. "We had to walk an extra half hour, and the other place doesn't have as good of food."

The argument must have been something serious for Jimmy to walk that far every day in the winter. They couldn't just change locations, either. Jimmy had his dumpster routes and begging spots. Moving into another territory could have stepped on toes and gotten him killed. That he'd rather walk than risk that supported Dwayne's assessment of him as smart.

Whatever he'd argued with the manager about must have been serious. Maybe even serious enough to get him killed.

WE DECIDED THE BEST WAY TO FIND OUT WHAT MIGHT BE happening behind the scenes at the mission was for me to volunteer. I wasn't selling enough cupcakes while sitting on the streets to cover what I was spending in fuel to stay warm. By volunteering at the shelter during the day, I'd actually come out ahead. I might even get a free meal out of it.

Heaven knew I needed one.

I called the mission, and the manager—whose name was

Lillian Ardis—practically gushed. People donated more food and money around the holidays but less time. They were short-handed.

Lillian didn't sound like someone who would beat a man to death…but then again, Jarrod didn't look like a man who would beat his wife, and he had.

Lillian met me at the door. And towered over me. She had to be nearly six feet tall, with broad shoulders and short-cropped blonde hair.

Her hand swallowed mine when we shook, but her smile made me feel welcome. Most people might have immediately written her off as a suspect. That's where I had an advantage over most people. I trusted no one.

She took me on a tour of the facilities. They had men and women's dormitory rooms, a spacious cafeteria, showers, and other smaller rooms where she explained they ran Alcoholics and Narcotics Anonymous meetings, as well as reading programs for the illiterate and even job match programs. Their mission had formed relationships with some of the local businesses who were willing to give a chance to the homeless who wanted to get back on their feet.

Her passion for it all made me suspect her argument with Jimmy had been over one of two things. Either he was doing something to hurt the work the mission was doing—which didn't seem likely given what I knew of him.

Or he'd found out she wasn't what she seemed.

CHAPTER 6

Lillian closed the door to the meeting room, and I felt my chance to ask her anything about Jimmy closing as well.

Once she settled me into my role, she'd be gone. I'd hesitated too long, trying to come up with the perfect segue. I wasn't a natural investigator like Nicole. I spent most of my time trying to *not* be noticed.

"You seem to do a lot to try to help them." I focused on controlling my voice. Our voices could give a lot away if we weren't careful. "Do you ever have problems with clients?"

Clients was what she'd told me they called the homeless they helped. It showed them respect.

"Do bears crap in the woods?" She rolled her eyes. "It's nothing compared to my last job, though. I used to work as a guard in a women's maximum-security prison." She smiled.

"Then I decided I'd rather try to keep people out of trouble rather than deal with them once they were already in it."

Even with my natural suspicion, I was having a hard time imagining what could have made her angry enough to kill. It had to be something Jimmy knew that would ruin her and the valuable work she felt she was doing. Maybe she'd crossed a line with a client.

"Do you ever have trouble maintaining your personal boundaries?"

There was a twitch it her cheek like the average person switched off and the prison guard—who couldn't react to anything the inmates said—switched on. "We have strict ethical codes that everyone, including volunteers, have to agree to."

Great. Now she suspected I was here to abuse a vulnerable population.

Or she's trying to distract you, Fear whispered. *Like an anglerfish luring its prey to the light before swallowing it whole.*

She motioned for me to follow her. "We're short-handed in the kitchen right now, so let's get you started."

In the kitchen, rather than out front, serving. It was a convenient way to keep me away from their homeless clients in case I turned out to be a problem and to also make sure I was watched by the other kitchen workers.

Normally I would have welcomed being behind the scenes,

but I'd hoped to talk to some of the clients and see how they felt about Lillian, see if there were any rumors about her.

Though that might be a better job for Dwayne. The other clients would trust him more, whereas I could see if the other volunteers had heard any arguments between Lillian and the clients.

Lillian pushed open a door. A burst of warm air nearly knocked me backward. If I'd been hoping to find a free place to stay warm, I'd found it. If I still had any extra pounds remaining, I'd sweat them away as well.

Two woman and one man worked inside, hardly enough to produce enough food for all the people I'd seen lining up.

Lillian pointed to the eldest woman, who wore a hair net over her curly dark hair. "Vy's our staff member. She'll give you your tasks."

She let the door swing shut, and it pushed me into the room.

Vy hustled toward me. "Thank the stars." She pushed a hair net and apron into my hands. "Ethan's peeling potatoes for the first time today, and at the rate he's going, we'll be serving Christmas dinner at Easter."

Ethan turned around. He had a dripping peeler in one hand, a half-naked potato in the other, and a look on his face that said he'd rather be anywhere else. He looked like the kind of man who should be at a baseball game, wearing a backwards hat and drinking a can of beer, rather than hanging out in a mission kitchen.

Being an outsider, Ethan might be more willing to talk. If he'd been here when Jimmy was still alive, he could be a good source.

Even if it meant standing shoulder to shoulder with a strange man. I'd just have to tell Fear to stuff it for a few hours.

I pulled the hair net on and tucked my braid up under it. "I can catch him up no problem."

Ethan held out the peeler toward me before I could tie on my apron.

Jumping right into questions about Lillian or the clients would likely make even him suspicious. I needed to figure out how to set him at ease with me first.

"How about you wash while I peel? I cook for a living." It wasn't a complete lie. I peeled plenty of carrots for my carrot cake cupcakes. I held out my other hand for his half-done potato. "No opportunity for peeling potatoes in your line of work, I'm guessing?"

You would have thought we were playing a game of hot potato with how fast Ethan tossed me the potato as well. "I'm a sanitation worker. No one wants me prepping food after I toss bags of garbage all day." He gave me a sheepish grin. "Well, except for the people here."

I returned his smile and set to work on the potatoes. He probably hadn't expected to end up in the kitchen any more than I had. I, at least, had food prep skills.

Thankfully, he'd given me a natural lead in. "Have you been volunteering long?"

"Less than two weeks. They had me cleaning at first, which was a better fit, but they had a couple of their regular kitchen volunteers call in sick today, so here I am."

He shrugged his shoulders like he couldn't understand it but wasn't going to argue. I didn't have to do any mental math to know that meant he'd started volunteering after Jimmy died. He wouldn't have been around to hear an argument between Jimmy and Lillian.

But pretending I didn't know might give me a lead-in to see if he'd heard any rumors about Jimmy or Lillian among the other volunteers. "Did you ever meet the man who was hit by the train?"

Ethan stopped scrubbing the potato he was working on. "I heard about that. It's really sad, but one of the things I've learned working here is that there are a lot of fights between clients."

I shifted my weight in his direction so that I could speak more softly and still be heard. Fear screamed so loudly in my head to back away that I could barely hear my own thoughts.

"I heard that he was fighting with the manager rather than one of the other clients."

"I've heard a few yelling matches since I've been volunteering here, but I still think it's more likely it was another client who killed him. Might have even been by accident. A lot of them have problems with anger and impulse control. You'll see once you've been here longer."

Dwayne and Carla had said it was strange to hear Lillian arguing with anyone. But it was possible they'd said that because they—unlike Ethan—were convinced it couldn't have been another homeless person who hurt Jimmy. They were looking for the killer to be someone other than another homeless person.

Before I could ask him anything more about what kinds of arguments he heard, Vy joined us to start mashing the potatoes that had already been boiled.

My subtlest attempt to find out what she knew about Jimmy was rebuffed with "I don't tolerate gossip in my kitchen."

It could have been my imagination, but she seemed to keep a closer eye on me for the rest of the evening, pairing up with me rather than allowing me to be alone with one of the other volunteers.

She even kept me to unload the dishwashers after all the other volunteers had left, as if she were afraid I'd accost one of them in the parking lot. She probably thought I was a reporter snooping around for a story. I'd tried to slide into conversation that I operated a cupcake food truck, only to realize from the look on her face that claiming to run a cupcake food truck in Michigan in December made me sound like a big, fat liar.

By the time we were done, the lights in the halls had been dimmed, and all the clients seemed to have gone to the dormitories. Vy disappeared before I could even collect up my coat and put on my gloves and scarf.

Walking down the halls, I could still hear the sounds of people talking and, from somewhere, music playing what sounded like jazz, but it felt strangely peaceful, like I'd stepped into a bubble.

The bubble burst as soon as I excited the building into the back parking lot and saw that my tires had been slashed.

CHAPTER 7

I clamped my hand around the building's door handle, not allowing it to swing shut. The person who'd slit my tires probably hadn't stuck around, but it wasn't worth taking the chance. I wasn't sure if the door would lock behind me if I let it close, trapping me out here alone.

One thing I knew at least—this wasn't Jarrod. He wouldn't bother wasting his time slashing tires. He'd go straight for me. Cutting a person's tires was either a warning or a delay tactic. There wasn't anything I was headed to after this, so I doubted it'd been meant to delay me. If it'd happened somewhere else, I would have guessed the perpetrator wanted to strand me far from help. But I could get help here even if I had ended up locked out.

That meant whoever did this most likely meant it as a warning. The only thing I could think of was that someone hadn't liked me asking questions about Jimmy. Then again, it was a pretty big leap for them to think I'd know that was why my tires were slashed. It didn't quite fit.

The adrenaline rushing through my body was making my limbs feel like they were pulsing and weak.

First I had to confirm that I wasn't panicking over nothing. Maybe I'd simply gotten a flat tire from a nail or wear. I leaned to the side so I could better see my other front tire.

It was flat as well.

I wasn't naïve enough to leave the door in order to check on my back tires. Not alone. Besides, if the front two were flat, the back two likely would be as well.

I backed into the building and pulled the door shut tightly behind me.

A security officer would have been the ideal person to ask to accompany me to check my other tires, but that wasn't an option. The mission had security officers outside during the day, but not at night. Once they'd reached their capacity for the night, they closed and locked the doors. If there was any trouble after that, the regular staff called the police. Or so Lillian had told me while briefing me quickly on protocol.

Even though the security staff was gone, Lillian or some other staff member should still be there.

I turned down the hallway that Lillian had pointed out as containing the offices. The door to the main office was still open, and the light was on.

Vy and Lillian sat together at a desk near the back. Their body language and the tone of their voices made me think they were fighting, but they were doing it too quietly for me to hear what they were saying.

Vy looked over. She must have caught my movement in her peripheral vision. "I thought you'd gone home."

"I tried to. I have a flat tire. I was too scared to change it on my own, just in case."

It sounded pathetic when I said it out loud, but it was true. Except the part where I wanted to change my tire. I had one spare and two—or more—flats.

Vy rolled her eyes, but Lillian got to her feet. "I'll come with you. If it's more than a simple flat, we'll have to write a report."

The skin on my arms felt like someone had trailed an ice cube along it. That seemed like a leap to make unless she already knew.

But the only way she could already know was if she'd been party to it.

She motioned for me to lead the way, but I held my ground. "If it's not a normal flat, what would it be?"

I tried to keep my voice controlled. Instead, it kicked up a little at the end, giving away my fear.

Though perhaps it would have sounded less natural if her statement hadn't scared me at all.

Lillian sighed. "Vandalism happens sometimes to vehicles in our parking lot. We need to extend our cameras out back, but we don't have the money in the budget yet. Are you parked in the back lot?"

I nodded. She set off, giving me no choice but to follow her.

She glanced back over her shoulder. "We have a higher-than-average rate of cars being broken into by clients who need money for their next fix. Or damaged by a client who was asked to leave. Even though we try to compensate volunteers for any damage done to their vehicles on our property, it's scary enough that most never return once something like this happens."

I hadn't even thought about the cost to repair my tires. Thankfully, it sounded like I didn't have to worry where the money for replacing them would come from.

I did wonder, though, whether Lillian was trying to make it easy or hard for me to leave by telling me that most volunteers who had their vehicles vandalized never returned.

On one hand, it could be her way of saying *It's okay if this isn't for you. It's not for most people.* Or it could be almost a taunt. *Are you going to be too weak to hack it, too?*

Neither would work on me. I was here with a specific purpose. I planned to stay until I'd accomplished it, but no longer.

That said, knowing how to interpret her words seemed important. Did she want me to stay, or did she want me to go?

I'd been poking around about Jimmy. If she'd killed him, she had a strong motive for wanting to get rid of me.

Her reaction if I pushed a little more might tell me where the truth lay, as well as helping me figure out if Jimmy had been banned from the mission.

I lengthened my stride so that I could walk beside her. "What kinds of things would get a person kicked out, for example?" I asked as casually as I could.

If she already thought I was a reporter, she might not even answer. For all I knew, that's what she and Vy were arguing about. Vy might have shared her suspicions about my motives, and Lillian might have responded by telling her that they were too short-handed to deny me a chance to volunteer. Or, more likely, their argument had nothing to do with me and everything to do with some other regular issue that came along with running a mission for the homeless.

The sidelong glance Lillian gave me made me think she was sizing me up. "Lots of things can get a client banned. Bringing weapons onto the premises. Assaulting security officers or other staff. For example."

Her echo of my words let me know that she didn't think I was a completely innocent volunteer. It'd been silly of me to think she would. She dealt with people who probably routinely lied to her. She'd probably gotten good at knowing who was being up-front and who wasn't.

Since I didn't yet have anything concrete about Jimmy and who might have wanted to kill him, I had to make sure she would allow me to come back another day. Assuming she'd fall for a part-truth.

We reached the door to the parking lot, and I stopped without opening it. "I heard that the man who died on the train tracks used to stay here. I was wondering if he killed himself because he wasn't allowed to stay here anymore. I like helping others, but I want to make sure I give my time to a place that helps and doesn't hurt."

Lillian's face did a weird transformation as I spoke, vacillating between tightening around her eyes that hinted at sadness and lowered eyebrows that made me think she was angry and about to kick me out, flat tires or no flat tires.

"We do the best we can, and sometimes we do have to evict people, but he wasn't one of them." She pushed open the door, and a rush of cold air hit me in the chest. "He tried to make money finding things in dumpsters and selling them. I encouraged him right up until he started trying to sell what he found to other clients in the building."

That sounded like it might have been the source of their fight, but I couldn't figure out why that would have caused a major disagreement.

Lillian must have been able to read the confusion on my face. Instead of stepping outside, she continued to stand in the doorway. "We can't allow clients to sell things to each other on mission property. He argued that he was helping them get phones and stuff they couldn't otherwise afford, but we can't bend the rules for anyone. It's a slippery slope." She nodded her head toward my truck. "Let's take a look at your tires. It's getting late."

The exhaustion in Lillian's voice—like she blamed herself a little bit even though she knew she shouldn't—made me think she hadn't had anything to do with Jimmy's death. It wasn't that kind of guilt. It sounded like the kind of guilt anyone in a mercy career felt when they lost one. They intellectually knew they couldn't save them all, but their hearts still wanted to.

Which meant that she also thought the police had been right that Jimmy killed himself. She didn't think it was a murder.

She hadn't killed him, and we were once again without a suspect for who had.

CHAPTER 8

All four of my tires had been slashed.

One tire might have been an angry resident who'd been banned from staying the night. All four felt like a targeted attack.

But whoever had done it hadn't left any sort of a message or warning. They didn't want me to know why they wanted to scare me away. They simply wanted me to leave and stop asking questions about Jimmy.

Lillian straightened up from examining the final tire. "Why don't you come back inside where it's warm? I'll call a tow truck and a cab to take you home."

The icy air seemed to freeze my lungs. I couldn't draw a full breath. She could call a cab for me, but I'd have nowhere to go if they hauled my truck away.

"I can just ride with the tow truck driver."

Lillian shook her head. "There's nothing open this time of night. The repair shop won't be able to replace your tires until morning. You might as well go straight home."

Nicole had figured out that I lived in my truck. She'd been the only one I'd ever admitted it to up until this point, not counting Dwayne and Carla, who'd figured it out on their own.

Now I had no choice but to trust that Lillian wouldn't turn me in to the health department. Because I wouldn't survive if I tried to sleep out on the streets tonight. I didn't have the right clothes, I didn't know where to find shelter, and I wasn't conditioned. My body still wanted to be home in sunny Florida.

I wrapped my arms around myself. "I don't have anywhere for the cab to take me."

Lillian glanced between me and the truck. "Oh."

She was probably wondering what a homeless person was doing volunteering at a mission. I could have fed her some line about how I was better off than most of her clients, and it would have been true. It also would have been a lie in that I wasn't there to help those less fortunate. I was there to try to right a wrong.

Lillian waved me back toward the mission. "I'll find you a cot if you don't mind sleeping in a dormitory room."

The dormitory rooms slept twenty to twenty-five people. I would have slept in a room twice that full so long as I didn't have to hunker down on the streets for the night. "I appreciate it."

She opened her mouth like she was finally going to ask why I was really there, but she closed it again before anything came out. Maybe it was going to work in my favor that she'd likely decided long ago not to ask too many questions of her clients or she'd end up hearing something she didn't want to know.

Lillian called someone on her cell as soon as we were back inside and asked them to set out a cot.

She led me down the hall to one of the women's dormitories. "Lights out in thirty minutes. Since you're an overnight guest, you're welcome to the hot meal we serve in the morning and use of the showers."

She left without another word and with a small piece of my dignity still intact. A very small piece.

I hadn't thought I was proud, but maybe I was a little. Until tonight, I hadn't considered myself homeless. I'd had my truck. That was my home.

Now, for tonight at least, I had nothing but the clothes on my back. And I felt smaller than I ever had.

I slunk into the room. At the far end, two female staff members assembled a cot with sheets and a pillow. The cot looked heavy and awkward to move. Men must not be allowed in the women's dormitories for any reason or two male staff members would have hauled it in.

I could look on the bright side. This might be the best night's sleep I'd had since leaving Fair Haven and Nicole's house. Jarrod wouldn't be able to get to me here because someone would notice a man in the woman's dorm.

I headed for the cot, then stopped. Halfway down the row, Carla sat propped up on a cot, playing on her phone, her feet crossed.

Feet that wore the same orange and green socks that Jimmy so proudly showed me a day before he died.

CHAPTER 9

M y feet and legs seemed to have forgotten how to walk.

The image of Jimmy lying across the tracks with bare feet and his shoes lying nearby had bothered me even before Nicole confirmed his death was murder. There was no reason I could think of for him to take his shoes off and leave his feet bare. And he'd been so proud of those socks. They'd represented something more than socks to him. They'd represented a healthy step he took to earn something again. They'd represented him trying to better his life.

To Carla, they represented something he'd kept for himself rather than giving to her. She'd also known about the train tracks as a spot Jimmy went, and Dwayne had been confused by it. He'd never heard of Jimmy going to the train tracks.

It was possible the train tracks were a spot she and Jimmy

went together. That night, they might have gotten into a fight, she'd pushed him, and then she'd staged it to look like he'd been drinking. She couldn't stand to leave those new socks behind, though, when her feet were cold.

I forced my feet to move forward. I had to stay here regardless. I had nowhere else to go.

Carla barely looked up as I passed by, giving me a brief nod in acknowledgment. She didn't seem surprised I was there. That could either mean she wasn't surprised because she already knew I was living out of my truck and might need a warmer place to sleep. It could also mean she knew I wouldn't be able to sleep in my truck because she'd slashed my tires.

I didn't like not knowing whether I was sleeping next to a garter snake or a viper.

I leaned toward thinking she was a viper. The one part that I couldn't make sense of was why Carla would have revealed the location of the body and then coerced me into helping investigate if she'd done it. Unless, of course, she thought that would make her look innocent, and we could find someone else who looked like they had a good motive to pin it on. Or perhaps she felt guilty after it was all over, and she couldn't stand leaving Jimmy's body there to decompose.

I sank down on my cot, untied my shoes, and shoved them underneath. I had to stay here overnight, but what I wanted to do was find Dwayne and present him with the evidence. There was no love lost between him and Carla. If he agreed with me that she'd likely done it, he'd say so and could tell the police.

Unfortunately, I couldn't get to Dwayne tonight. I wasn't allowed into the men's dormitories any more than men were allowed into the women's.

All I could do was wait for morning…and try to sleep in a room with a woman who might be a murderer.

I DREAMED THAT CARLA FIGURED OUT I KNEW SHE KILLED JIMMY and she tried to smother me with a pillow. After that, I couldn't sleep at all.

I was up before anyone else and went out into the hallway to wait for Dwayne.

If my luck was changing, I might be done with all of this today. As soon as my truck was fixed, I'd pick a new town and head on. This one had gotten too complicated. Too many people knew me and knew that I lived in my truck.

The looks some of the men gave me as they passed by made my skin want to crawl off my body and go into hiding.

By the time Dwayne came out, my hands were shaking, and I couldn't get them to stop. I motioned frantically for him to follow me around the corner.

He didn't hesitate.

"Did you find out what they were fighting about?" Dwayne

asked almost before we were far enough away to avoid being overheard.

I peeked around the corner to make sure no one was coming our way. Too much more of this cloak-and-dagger stuff and I was going to have an ulcer before I turned forty.

"I don't think it was the manager who killed him." I glanced around the corner again. Even though there was no one around, my body wouldn't shut off the adrenaline rush. It made me jumpy and queasy all at the same time. "Carla has Jimmy's new socks. I think she took them off his feet after she killed him."

Dwayne's skin turned a shade of yellow-green I'd only seen before on an over-ripe avocado. "She wouldn't do that. She loved him."

Yeah. Jarrod claimed to love me, too, but he still beat me. "It could have been an accident during an argument. I got the impression that their relationship was a rocky one."

It was only a guess. The way Dwayne's posture drooped told me I'd been right.

"They fought. Mostly 'cause Jimmy'd stopped drinking and wanted to try to find a way to get off the streets, and Carla couldn't seem to stay sober longer than a week." He shook his head like he didn't want to give my suggestion a chance to settle in. "Their fights never got physical. Never."

Never that he saw. Most abuse happened without witnesses. "This could have been the first time, especially if Jimmy wanted to move on and leave her behind. Carla admits she has a temper."

Dwayne slumped back against the wall and tightened his ponytail. "I still can't believe it. 'Sides, Carla knew Jimmy didn't drink beer. She knew it even better than me. I met Jimmy at the AA meetings here when we was both trying to get sober. Carla was his drinking buddy when he wasn't."

I had to admit that was a good defense. But maybe I could explain that away, too. "Was she a beer drinker?"

Dwayne nodded slowly.

"Then maybe it was what she had with her at the time, and she didn't have the money for something else."

"She didn't have to lead us to Jimmy's body."

I'd had half the night to think up possible reasons for why she might have. "How did she know he went to the train tracks when you didn't?"

Dwayne pushed away from the wall. "We got to at least give her a chance to explain how she got his socks. This is America, and people are supposed to be innocent until proven guilty."

I couldn't take what I'd learned to the police myself, so that left me with no choice but to go along with Dwayne until he was convinced as well. "You're right. We should at least talk to her first."

WE FOUND CARLA IN THE CAFETERIA. CARLA AND DWAYNE BOTH scarfed their eggs and sausage down almost without chewing, but I had a hard time swallowing any of it. I should have eaten as much as they'd give me, glad for a free meal. The tension seemed to block my throat. Dwayne kept eyeing Carla, Carla kept eyeing me, and I kept eyeing Dwayne, wondering how he was going to broach the topic once we were done.

By the time we finished eating, Carla's shoulders were tight, and she carried her arms close to her sides, hands fisted like she wanted to punch someone and couldn't.

We headed as a unit to return our plates.

"What did you find out?" Carla's words came out in a loud hiss.

Another man returning his dirty plate glanced in her direction.

"Not here," Dwayne whispered.

Carla must have assumed I'd found something that would point to Lillian as Jimmy's killer because she clamped her mouth shut so hard it looked like someone had literally glued her lips together.

Dwayne led the way out the back door and into an alley behind the mission. If he noticed my truck wasn't parked there, he didn't say anything. Carla knew I'd spent the night, but he didn't.

He let Carla enter the alleyway first. It was a dead end, blocked off on the opposite side by a high, wired fence. He moved into the middle of the end we'd entered and stopped.

Carla stopped and turned around. She must have sensed we weren't following her anymore.

Her eyes narrowed to match the thin line of her lips. "What're you doing, Dwayne?"

I instinctively backed up a step. It was like watching two boxers circle each other in the ring, and I didn't want to be anywhere close if it came to blows.

Dwayne had made it clear that he didn't want to talk to her until we were off mission property. *No fighting* was one of the rules, and he wanted to be able to continue sleeping there. At the time, I'd thought he meant verbal arguments. Now I wasn't so sure.

If it'd still been dark out, I would have pulled out my phone to check for security cameras. Based on the fact that this was where Dwayne chose to confront Carla, my guess was there weren't any.

He widened his stance a little more. "Show me your socks."

Something flickered across her face. If I hadn't been so familiar with it, I might not have been able to figure out what it was. But Fear and I were so close I could never mistake the evidence of his presence.

"I'm not showing you my socks," she said. "They're nothing special, and it's cold out here."

Dwayne took a step toward her. "Just pull up your pant leg."

Carla didn't move. She glanced back over her shoulder toward the fence, as if looking for an escape route. The chain-link fence was too high to leap over, and the links were too small to provide a decent handhold.

When she turned back around, she looked at me, not at Dwayne. Her gaze could have frozen a boiling pot. She knew I had to have seen the socks last night.

She leaned down and pulled up a pant leg. The garish socks were easy to recognize.

Dwayne was shaking his head again in that way that made me think he was trying to prevent the truth from sinking in. "I told her you couldn't have done it."

She crossed her arms over her chest. "I didn't do nothing other than take his socks, and those were mine by right as his wife. He was dead when I found him."

"Tell me what happened, then," Dwayne said. "Convince me you didn't have nothing to do with this."

He'd had a much softer tone when he'd defended her earlier, but he must have known she wouldn't admit the truth if he didn't push her. It was likely why he'd asked me to stay quiet and let him do the talking. I couldn't push Carla the way he could and get away with it.

"There's nothing to tell. I found him just like you saw, took his socks 'cause he didn't need them anymore and he should've given them to me in the first place, and then went to tell you I was worried about him."

Then they'd come to find me, in part because I had a vehicle and, in part, because Carla already knew what they'd find. They'd both sounded afraid the police would blame them. It's why they wanted me to call it in.

"Did you put the beer near him?" Dwayne asked.

I almost corrected him that someone had poured beer all over Jimmy's clothes to make it smell like he'd been drinking, but I clamped my lips shut. Carla already didn't like me. If I interrupted to correct Dwayne, she might lash out. Or shut down.

Carla shook her head. "I'm not stupid. If I'd wanted to stage it to look like he'd been drinking, I wouldn't've used beer."

Dwayne's stance had relaxed enough that he seemed willing to take Carla's word for it. He didn't want her to be guilty.

But he hadn't asked one of the most important questions.

Dwayne moved aside enough to make it clear he wasn't blocking the alley anymore. "You shouldn't have taken his socks, no matter if they were yours now or not. It makes you look guilty."

He wasn't going to ask. Anger or no anger from Carla, I had to ask it. Dwayne had come at her strongly, but I wasn't sure if that was the right approach for me. Maybe if I made my question softer, she wouldn't jump me in the dark one night.

"If the police ever find out, you'll need to explain how you knew where Jimmy would be to look for him," I said. "They're not going to believe it was one of his regular spots since Dwayne didn't know about it."

Carla stepped toward me. "You better not tell the police." Her voice rose to a yell.

Dwayne moved toward me, presumably letting Carla know he wasn't going to allow her to hit me to shut me up. "She's not saying she's gonna tell the police. She'd just saying that's something they'll want to know. It's something I want to know, too. I walked Jimmy's route with him all the time, and he never went to the tracks. Too much drinking happened there."

"It wasn't one of his spots." Carla's lips turned down. "I didn't go looking for him. I went to drink where I knew he wouldn't find me. But there he was."

If Jimmy never went there, then it wasn't a spot they were likely to have a fight that accidentally led to his death.

Even though Carla couldn't provide anything that proved she was innocent, that one detail made me believe her.

The truth might also help us figure out who actually killed him.

"If Jimmy never went there, then someone moved his body from where he really died. The person who did it knows that people go there to drink, but didn't know Jimmy wasn't drinking anymore."

"I told you I thought the manager Jimmy fought with did it. She knows all about our spots, but she wouldn't know what Jimmy liked to drink."

"She knew Jimmy was attending AA, though." Dwayne's voice had lost all its confrontation. "I think we're looking at the wrong person."

"Isabel?" a man's voice said from the end of the alley.

It wasn't Jarrod's voice, but it was one I'd heard before. Remembering and identifying voices had never been a strength of mine. I got people wrong on the phone repeatedly unless I knew them well.

I turned around.

Ethan.

He stepped one foot further into the alley. "I heard yelling. Are you okay?"

The look on his face as he glanced at Carla told me he'd heard more than yelling. He'd overheard enough to think that Carla might be a killer.

CHAPTER 10

Standing in the alley between Ethan and Carla felt a bit like watching a flame creep closer to a big puddle of gasoline. If Carla figured out that he'd been eavesdropping, I had no idea what she might do.

"Why don't you two go?" I said softly to Dwayne.

I couldn't tell if he knew what I was worried about or if he just didn't want to talk anymore about who'd hurt Jimmy. Either way, he left the alleyway, and Carla followed his lead.

Leaving me to figure out how much Ethan knew and whether or not that made him a threat to Carla. And, in a way, a threat to me. If he went to the police with what he'd heard, he'd tell them everything, including who was in the alley with Carla. He didn't know my fake last name, but the police could get it from Lillian. I'd had to give it to her to volunteer.

My name in the system shouldn't lead Jarrod to me. He didn't have any way of knowing I was using the name Isabel Addington. But the police would know it was a fake name if they ran it. If they then asked for my fingerprints, everyone would know who I really was.

I couldn't let that happen.

"Are you okay?" Ethan asked again.

"Everything's fine." I smiled at him with the smile that always fooled people. "I didn't expect you'd be back this morning. You were here so late last night."

Ethan's gaze followed Dwayne and Carla as they left. "I'm here whenever I have time off."

He didn't come into the alley with me. Instead, he seemed to be waiting for me to come out. I needed to go back inside and find out when I could pick up my truck anyway.

I joined Ethan.

We walked in silence most of the way back to the building. He sneaked a glance at me three times, like he wanted to broach the topic but didn't know how.

We couldn't get back into the building from the rear door without a code, so we headed toward the sidewalk that led to the front.

Two paces before we rounded the corner of the building, Ethan stopped and reached out a hand in my direction, like he was trying to stop me from going any further. "I didn't mean to, but I heard some of the conversation you were having with them."

Some. Not all. Maybe there was still a chance he'd only heard the part where we were trying to figure out who might have killed Jimmy and not the part where we were basically accusing Carla of having done it.

He ducked his head down to make sure his gaze held mine. "You need to tell the police."

My hopes deflated faster than a failed soufflé. "There's nothing to tell." Great. Now not only was I lying, but I also sounded like Carla. My dad might have been right after all that the people you spend time with influence who you are. "They were friends of the man who was killed on the train tracks. We don't think it was an accident, and we're trying to figure out who would have wanted to hurt him."

"I was standing there for a while." He held up his hands as if to stop the reprimand he was sure was coming. "I know no one likes being spied on, but I was trying to decide if someone was in trouble."

Someone was in trouble. And I wasn't entirely sure whether it was me or Carla.

I believed her story. There were too many things that she probably would have done differently if she'd been the one to kill Jimmy, by accident or intentionally.

Unfortunately for her, there was also enough evidence to make her a prime suspect. Given that she was homeless and would be given a public defender who would probably also think she was guilty, her chances of acquittal if she were charged with Jimmy's murder were slim.

While I didn't like Carla, I had liked Jimmy. I didn't want to know that his real murderer was walking around, enjoying their life, while someone else paid for their crime. If nothing else, my innate sense of justice wouldn't allow it. My dad had taught me that we had to stand up for what was right. I hadn't done that perfectly in my life, but I also couldn't completely shake it.

I'd suffered for years while Jarrod benefitted. It hadn't been fair then, and it wasn't fair now.

"I don't know what you heard, but I think you probably misunderstood."

He raised an eyebrow as if to say *Do you think I'm stupid?* "She has the dead man's socks. She drinks beer, and he didn't, but they found beer with his body. And they were married and on the outs."

Okay, so he'd heard everything perfectly. He'd been standing there for almost the whole conversation. Which, frankly, was a bit creepy, his explanation notwithstanding. Though my problem with it was likely due to how I'd lived under the constant threat of Jarrod watching me and tracking me. I wasn't sure how a normal person would have felt. They probably would have been grateful Ethan cared enough about others to make sure everything was kosher.

I forced myself to meet his gaze without flinching. "She didn't do this."

"You don't know who did this. That's for the police to decide." He tapped his temple. "Any information you have about it should go to them."

It was that divide in thinking again that I'd noticed with Nicole. She'd also assumed that all police were good and unbiased. They weren't. Carrying a badge didn't guarantee that someone was a good person.

The police in Fair Haven had been mostly good and honest and tried to do their jobs with as little bias as possible. I didn't know what the police here would be like.

The decision about what to do settled on my shoulders like I'd stacked bricks there. "The police don't always get it right."

Ethan's gaze shifted. For a second, I thought he was going to put his hand on my shoulder. "No. No one always gets its right, no matter how hard we try. But I figure we have to trust the professionals to steer us in the best way. I trust my priest to tell me what penance I need to do for my sins, and I trust my dentist when my teeth hurt. You know what I mean?"

I did. But I'd also once had an unnecessary root canal done because my dentist made a mistake. "I'll think about it. I don't want to point a finger at her if she didn't do it. I promise we'll"—I was careful not to say *I'll*—"take any information we find to the police eventually."

His expression changed, almost like the skin around his eyes turned to stone. "Not eventually. If you don't go to the police with this, I will."

CHAPTER 11

I couldn't take what I knew to the police, but I couldn't let Ethan do it, either. The police might even think my reluctance to share what I knew meant I'd been a party to the crime.

Which meant I needed to stall. Stalling was a great tactic. If you stalled them long enough, most people gave up or forgot because something more important in their lives would come along. If nothing else, it would give me a chance to decide if skipping town now was the better way to go.

Technically, I had nothing holding me here. Christmas was only a few days away, and my catering gigs were completed.

Nothing, that is, except a strange sense of kinship with people who also had no home and seemed to have the world against them.

I slumped my shoulders forward and allowed my head to droop with it. It was my I'm-sorry-and-I'm-not-a-threat pose. "Will you give me a chance to try to convince her to go in and talk to the police herself? They might give her some leniency if she does that. If she killed him, I don't think it was premeditated."

Ethan's jaw clenched, then unclenched. "That's fair. Twenty-four hours. If she hasn't agreed by then, she won't."

I almost lost my faked submissive look. I hadn't expected him to actually go for it. I wouldn't have. Asking her to turn herself in gave her forewarning and a chance to disappear. Disappearing wouldn't be in her long-term benefit—it'd make her look guiltier —but Carla didn't seem like someone who'd care. She also didn't seem like someone who would think about it logically. She'd react on instinct.

Ethan and I walked the rest of the way in together. Just before we parted ways, he tapped his watch as if to remind me of the ticking clock on Carla's freedom.

Somehow his pushing me to turn over what I knew to the police solidified my belief that she was innocent. Being pushed forced me to pick a side and defend it. It was probably a psychological phenomenon that had some name my dad would have known from all his reading, but I didn't.

What I did know was that now, instead of trying to sell a handful of cupcakes to people two days before Christmas, I had to try to find Dwayne and Carla and come up with a plan to figure out who'd really killed Jimmy within the next twenty-four hours.

THE DAY WAS HALF GONE BY THE TIME MY TRUCK HAD TIRES AND I was back behind the wheel. I knew Jimmy's basic dumpster diving route, give or take a few dumpsters, but I didn't know where Dwayne or Carla spent their days. I decided to go to one of the spots where they found me before and hope one of them showed up.

By the time three o'clock came, I'd sold more cupcakes than I thought I would thanks to last-minute Christmas shoppers, but Dwayne and Carla were nowhere around.

All I could think was that they expected me to be back volunteering at the mission that night and planned to meet up with me there.

Either that or they'd both already vanished and left me looking stupid and complicit.

I headed back for the mission. A few people were already standing in line for a space, but there were so few that it was easy to see as I drove by that Dwayne and Carla weren't there yet.

I pulled around back and parked my truck, under the nearest

streetlamp to the door this time. Even though it wasn't dark yet by any means, the winter sky had that dull gray look to it that seemed to make the sun disappear long before it actually set.

I didn't miss hurricane season in Florida, but I did miss the year-round sunshine.

Dwayne and Carla stepped out of the alleyway.

I'd debated whether or not to tell them about Ethan's threat. I'd decided not to because I wasn't entirely sure Carla wouldn't jump him in the parking lot if I did. Since he'd been at the shelter this morning, he'd hopefully gone home by now, but I didn't want it on my conscience if he hadn't.

I motioned them back to the alleyway. Lillian had told me the back didn't have cameras. There were cameras all around the rest of the mission.

"We need to think again about who might have wanted Jimmy dead," I said once we were all halfway back and—hopefully—safe from eavesdroppers. I wasn't taking chances again.

"So you believe me now?" Carla's voice was half surly and half genuinely hopeful, as if she wasn't used to being believed.

What had brought her and Jimmy to this kind of life? It wasn't the right time to ask, but there had to be a story behind it —probably a sad one. One involving a mortgage they couldn't pay or the death of a child.

"I do." I pointed at her feet. "But we have a problem. The police are going to look at you eventually because you were his wife. If they find your DNA on the bottles or on his shoes, the only way you're not going to prison is if we can show them someone else was more likely the person who killed him."

Carla blinked rapidly. "Dwayne said you were gonna help me eventually. I didn't believe him."

I almost thought I heard her say *thank you* under her breath, but I wasn't entirely sure. Just like I wasn't sure whether she was trying not to cry or the cold was making her eyes water the way it was mine.

Either way, getting back to the problem we had to solve would make the situation less awkward for both of us. "I was thinking we need to make a list of everyone who knew Jimmy was a recovering alcoholic."

Dwayne shook his head. "We were talking about that, too. Most people think anyone who's homeless is also a drunk. They might not have known nothing about Jimmy's past."

So not necessarily someone who knew Jimmy. Carla and Dwayne were also convinced it wasn't another member of the homeless community, and I was sure it wasn't Lillian. What did that leave us?

All I knew about Jimmy beyond that was that he liked my cupcakes and that he dumpster dove, looking for things he could fix up and sell.

"What if he found something in a dumpster that he shouldn't have? The person who threw it there could have caught him picking through the garbage and been afraid he'd figure something out."

"Or he could have tried to talk to them about it if he knew who put it there." Dwayne sneaked a not-so-subtle glance at Carla. "He was a good guy. He was always wanting to give people a second chance."

Confronting someone about a potential crime seemed foolhardy to me, but I was a coward at heart. I hadn't stood up to anyone in my life when it really counted.

I checked my watch. Dwayne and Carla would need to get in line soon or they wouldn't have a meal and a place to sleep tonight. My truck wasn't big enough for all three of us to sleep in, and I certainly didn't have enough food in it to feed me, let alone them. I'd even sold out most of my cupcakes for today— though that wasn't saying much since I'd only been able to toss together a hasty two batches once I got my truck back.

Dark would be here soon, too, making retracing Jimmy's steps extra difficult.

"What about if we meet tomorrow morning to travel Jimmy's route? We can see what kinds of things are dumped and what businesses or apartments dump there. It won't give us a name, but it's a place to start."

Given how short we were on time, I was going to grasp even that tiny straw for a beginning.

We agreed to meet up the next day immediately after they finished breakfast.

Two hours later, I was in the kitchen, loading the first batch of dishes into one of the industrial dishwashers when I heard shouting.

Carla shouting.

Carla's yelling got louder. Vy turned to face the kitchen door as if considering whether she should go out into the hallway.

I twisted the dishcloth I was holding. *You need to leave this place,* Fear insisted. *And not come back. This isn't your problem.*

It wasn't my problem. But I'd made it my problem. Beyond the fact that I'd liked Jimmy, beyond the fact that they'd given me tips on finding places to park, and beyond the fact that I felt a sense of kinship with them because none of us had homes.

Beyond everything else, they'd gone hunting for their friend who went missing.

When I'd disappeared, there was no one who cared enough about me to even notice, let alone search for me and try to figure out what happened.

Maybe that said something about Jimmy in comparison to me. I'd been very isolated. Maybe it said something about Dwayne and even Carla and the kind of people they were. Maybe it was both.

But they were doing what I wish I'd had someone to do for me—believe that I mattered and care what happened to me.

Vy turned back toward me. "Sometimes these things happen. I'll check with the office to make sure the police have been called."

She turned her back to me and pulled her cell phone from her pocket.

"I didn't do it." Carla must have been closer to the kitchen now. I could make out words. "He was dead when I found him."

My legs gave out, and I caught myself on the edge of the counter just in time.

I glanced at Vy. She didn't need to call the office to make sure the police had been called. The sick feeling in my stomach told me the police were the reason Carla was yelling in the first place.

They'd come to arrest her.

Ethan hadn't kept his word. He'd gone to the police after all. There was no other way they could have decided to arrest her.

Hopefully I was jumping to conclusions. They might simply be trying to take her in for questioning because she was Jimmy's spouse. Carla wasn't the calmest woman. She might have panicked. She might think they were blaming her for Jimmy's murder when they weren't. Yet.

She'd make things worse for herself by overreacting—especially if for some reason Dwayne wasn't there to calm her down.

I dropped the dish towel on the counter and headed for the door while Vy's back was still turned.

I hurried for the cafeteria. It was suspiciously emptier than it should have been. Many of the clients seemed to have slinked away, not wanting to be part of the scene taking place. Others stared openly, while a few didn't even seem to be aware of the commotion happening. They were either lost in their own minds—where the real world meant little—or they were hoping that by avoiding eye contact they'd also go unnoticed.

A few feet away from the door, Carla stood in front of two police officers, gesturing wildly, her arms looking as if they'd detach from her body at any moment from the sheer force of her movements.

The fact that they'd sent two officers hinted that my hopes might be wrong. This might, in fact, be an arrest.

Carla's gaze landed on me.

She bulldozed between the two officers. One of them stumbled to the side, and the other grabbed him, keeping him upright.

The look on Carla's face reminded me of the way Jarrod looked before some of my worst beatings. I instinctively raised my arms to protect my face.

Carla slammed me into the wall, and pain ricocheted through my body.

"You lied to me."

Slam.

I let my body go limp. It was like how the drunk driver in an accident was always hurt less than the person they crashed into because their bodies were more relaxed. I'd figured out how to turn my body into a ragdoll a long time ago.

"You pretended like you were gonna help me."

Slam.

My body took the blow, but my heart felt it. She *had* been fighting back tears in the alley yesterday. She wasn't used to people believing her and being willing to help her. She'd taken the risk on trusting me, and now she thought I'd betrayed her.

I opened my mouth to tell her it wasn't me. She slammed me into the wall again, and the air rushed from my lungs.

Then she was being hauled back. The officers each had ahold of one of her arms. She turned her fury on them, cussing.

Without her pinning me to the wall, I sank to the ground. Everything around me spun.

Someone knelt down next to me. I hoped it was Dwayne so I could explain. When my eyes focused, I realized it was Lillian.

She didn't touch me, probably because she was too well-trained when it came to not touching her clients, even platonically. "Do you need me to call an ambulance?"

My whole body ached, but I wasn't going to a hospital. Not even if she'd caused internal bleeding. Hospitals cost money that I didn't have. "I've survived worse."

Lillian glanced back over her shoulder. I followed her gaze.

With the officers gone, there was a buzz in the room, like everyone was talking in whispers. Too many of them stared in our direction.

Lillian focused back on me. "We appreciate that you've helped out, but I think it might be best if you found somewhere else to volunteer. Tires can be replaced…"

She didn't have to finish her sentence. I knew. Tires could be replaced, but I only had one life. No one would trust me now. I was a snitch in their eyes. My tires might not be the only thing damaged next time.

The only way to redeem this was to find Dwayne and continue with our plan. We could still retrace Jimmy's regular route together. Dwayne knew it better than anyone.

Anything we found would help prove Carla was innocent. And it'd also prove me innocent. It'd show them that I hadn't turned Carla in.

That shouldn't have mattered. I didn't really owe them anything, not even loyalty. Carla had threatened and coerced me almost the whole time I'd known her.

But I wanted to be the kind of person others searched for when they went missing. I wanted to be the kind of person who searched for others if they went missing. I didn't want to be able to vanish again without someone missing me.

Right now, the only people who'd miss me happened to be

two homeless people. I'd made sure to distance myself from Nicole enough that she wouldn't even realize I was gone.

Maybe I should say *one homeless person* since right now Carla would only come looking for me to beat me up.

I crawled to my feet. Lillian didn't offer me a hand. It seemed harsh, but I could understand. In her own way, she couldn't afford to make connections, either.

Dwayne didn't seem to be anywhere in the room. But he should have been, since it was meal time.

Given what had just happened, if I were him, I'd be trying to walk to the station in pursuit of Carla. It was a long walk, but it was my best guess. If he wasn't at the police station, I'd have to find a way to inconspicuously stake out the mission until he came back.

Lillian walked me out. She must have been more worried for my safety than I'd realized.

She watched until I was in my truck, engine started and doors locked.

I headed in the direction of the police station. I wasn't far down the street before my headlights illuminated a man in a long, raggedy coat walking along the sidewalk. I recognized Dwayne's blond ponytail sticking out from under his winter hat.

I put on my hazard lights and slowed down next to him. I rolled down my window. "Hop in. I'll give you a ride there."

The look he gave me was colder than the air rushing in

through my open window. He thought I'd turned Carla in, too. "I'd rather walk."

"I didn't tell the police about the socks."

His expression said *Sure, and I'm the President of the United States.* "You were the only one who knew."

I hadn't been the only one, but Ethan was still volunteering at the shelter. If I revealed that it'd been him, he might not be safe there, either. It wouldn't be right of me to put him in danger to earn back Dwayne's trust.

"We need to stick to the plan, now more than before." I felt like I was having to scream to be heard. I threw my truck into park, turned it off, and jumped out. I scurried after him. "We can still find evidence of who else might have killed Jimmy. It'll help her."

Dwayne stopped. He turned to face me. "The police aren't going to look into anything we find now, and a public defender won't have time, even if they believed her."

"I can call my lawyer friend. She sometimes does pro bono work."

The words were out before I could stop them, and then I couldn't grab them back. I had no right to bring Nicole into this. And to offer up her services for free. Though Carla's case was exactly the kind of thing she thrived on—an innocent person, falsely accused, with all the evidence pointing toward them.

Dwayne raised an eyebrow. "Your promises don't mean a lot anymore."

I stepped back. This wasn't fixable. They weren't ever going to believe me, probably not even if I told them about Ethan. They'd just think I should have worked harder to stop him or that I should have warned them.

They'd be right. I should have warned them. I hadn't wanted Carla to run, but I should have warned them. Trying to protect them from the truth had been a mistake on my part.

A mistake that was going to cost me my only connections in this city. It was stupid of me, but with all the hassle they'd brought into my life, at least I hadn't felt so alone.

Maybe alone was all I'd ever be. Maybe alone was better.

But I couldn't leave Carla to the wolves. I bore some responsibility for her arrest. I'd pointed out that she'd taken Jimmy's socks, and Ethan overheard.

I fished a piece of paper and a pen out of my purse. I wrote down Nicole's information. "This is her name and number. You can tell her you got it from me or not. But I think you should call her."

Dwayne learned backward. His gaze flickered from the paper in my hand to my face and back again. He snatched the paper from my fingers and shoved it into his coat pocket. "I'll think about it. Whatever happens now, Carla and I will handle on our own. Without you."

Dwayne refused to even allow me to drive him to the police station. He was probably afraid I would have spent the drive trying to convince him to continue with our plan to go back along Jimmy's route and check the dumpsters.

I wouldn't have.

The idea had been a long shot. It'd been the only shot we had, but they'd now both made it clear that I wasn't welcome anymore. I hadn't really been their ally. I'd been convenient.

I tried not to let it sting, but for once, Fear's voice in my head was drown out by the memory of Jarrod's telling me I was worthless and unlovable and lucky he put up with me because no one else would.

I drove around for half an hour despite how wasteful it was. I couldn't stay in any of the places Jimmy, Dwayne, or Carla had told me about. If the police released Carla for whatever reason, she might be angry enough to hunt me down.

This wasn't how I'd expected this week to go. I'd almost been looking forward to serving Christmas Eve and Christmas Day meals at the homeless shelter. At least I wouldn't have been alone for the holidays.

I gave myself a shake. I'd been alone for most of the last year. Even before that, living under Jarrod's control hadn't been emotionally fulfilling. I was better off alone. I knew how to be alone. I could handle this.

The first order of business was a safe place to park for the night.

I headed to the opposite side of town from the mission and the areas Dwayne and Carla frequented. It was mostly subdivisions, but there were a few stores with parking lots in the back that would keep me off the street and mostly out of sight.

I pulled into the lot of a second-hand clothing store.

The problem with parking in a new spot was that I didn't know the routines—how early did the first employee arrive, did they have a security company hired to patrol the area, did they have security cameras?

While I couldn't control for the first two, I could go back to my method for checking for cameras. Since it was already dark out, it was as easy as pulling out my cell phone.

I slipped out of the cab of my truck. I didn't see any pinpricks of light with my naked eye. If I went to the camera screen on my phone and saw one on the screen, I'd know the business had an infrared security camera. The trick had saved me more than once from arousing suspicion by showing up repeatedly on a security video.

I checked my screen. No red dots.

I hit the home button on my phone and slid it back into my jacket pocket. This was probably the safest place for me to camp for the night that I was going to find on short notice.

I headed toward the back of my truck but stopped. Security cameras. Why hadn't I thought of it before?

Maybe we didn't have to search the dumpsters to see if Jimmy found something that got him killed. We might be able to get lucky and one of the nearby businesses caught something on surveillance video. A lot of businesses now had cameras guarding the backs of their stores.

The police wouldn't have thought to check for security cameras along Jimmy's regular route because they believed he'd died in the train yard. Businesses didn't look at their footage unless the police asked for it or they'd been robbed.

And Jimmy wouldn't have adapted his route to avoid cameras. He must not have known how to check for them because Dwayne and Carla didn't seem to know how to check for them. They would have offered up that trick as a bribe to get me to help them if they had.

Unfortunately, it also meant they'd probably think I was making it up. If they'd even listen to me in the first place. If I could find Dwayne. That was a lot of *ifs*. The police weren't going to let me visit Carla, setting aside the fact that I didn't think I was brave enough to go into a police station and try.

I drove back toward the police station. Even with how long I'd been roaming around the city, Dwayne probably wouldn't have reached the station yet. It had to be a good ninety-minute walk.

He wasn't anywhere along the route that I took.

I turned back. They wouldn't have let him see Carla any more than they would have let anyone see Carla. Only her lawyer would have access to her. That meant that if Dwayne had reached the police station, he'd be sitting in the lobby, waiting to find out if they arrested her or set her free for now.

All I had to do was stick my head inside.

I wouldn't have to talk to any police officers.

No matter how many times I repeated that to myself on the drive back to the station, my heart wouldn't slow down. It was like it was trying to run away from the station as fast as I was driving toward it.

I parked in the parking lot and headed for the door.

Fear had given up on screaming at me that I was heading into a place full of people who'd turn me over to Jarrod and had instead moved down into my stomach, where he seemed intent on making me sick.

It's just the lobby, I reminded myself. *You don't have to go any further than the lobby.*

If Dwayne wasn't there, I'd be reduced to hoping he showed back up at the shelter. But the longer we waited to check for cameras, the more likely it would be that any evidence would be taped over. Most places didn't keep their tapes for longer than two weeks.

Two weeks was tomorrow night—Christmas Eve. If we didn't go tonight, we might lose our chance.

My arm was so weak as I grabbed the station door that it took me two tries to pull it open.

Three people sat in the lobby.

None of them were Dwayne.

I backed out. One step outside the door, I gulped in a huge breath of cold air.

In hindsight, it was almost better Dwayne hadn't been there. I might not have had enough breath to talk to him, and he wouldn't have wanted to come with me. That would have only drawn more attention to us.

All I could do now was drive slowly back toward the mission again. Ideally, I'd see him on the way.

If not, I'd have to get someone to let me in and then find someone else who could go into the men's dormitories to look for him.

———

I'D EXPECTED TO HAVE TO TRY CALLING TO GET SOMEONE TO LET

me into the mission, but there were extra cars in the mission parking lot when I arrived, and the front doors were unlocked.

A sign taped to the front door said the weekly AA meeting had been moved to a new room. The meeting had to be why the doors were open when they usually locked after the mission reached capacity.

Dwayne had said that he and Jimmy met at an Alcoholics Anonymous meeting. With everything that had been happening, he probably needed a meeting to keep from relapsing. I might find him there, and that's why I hadn't been able to find him at the police station or anywhere along the route. He might have turned back after I talked to him, remembering what day it was.

Thanks to the room change, I knew exactly where to go.

The halls were empty. The clients would be in the dormitories by now or taking their turn in the showers.

The door to the room where the meeting was being held was closed. I checked the handle. It wasn't locked.

But I didn't feel right intruding. I wasn't in recovery. I didn't belong there, listening to their private stories.

Based on what I could see through the window, this was the only exit other than out a window. If Dwayne was inside, he'd have to pass by me.

I leaned against the wall and waited. Ten minutes passed, then twenty. Finally, the door swung open and people filtered out.

I was so busy watching for Dwayne that I jumped when someone said my name.

Ethan stood in front of me. Another person came out, and he moved to the side, out of the flow of human traffic. "I heard about what happened tonight. I didn't think you'd still be here."

I wanted to say *No thanks to you.* Except my brain had been trained to not say what I was thinking. I couldn't get the words to come out.

Besides, if Dwayne wasn't in the meeting, I'd need a man to go into the dormitories looking for him. I couldn't afford to anger Ethan.

I leaned to the side slightly to make sure I could still see everyone leaving the room. "I need to find someone. The man I was with in the alley. He has a long, blond ponytail." I reached my hand up to my own braid. "His name is Dwayne."

"Yeah, I've seen him in meetings a couple of times, but he wasn't here tonight. I'm almost two weeks sober now." Ethan smiled, and his rounded cheeks gave him a weirdly cherubic appearance. "I was getting so bad that I was drunk at work even, while driving my truck. Now I'm counting off the days to my one-month chip."

That felt like something I should congratulate him for, but I wasn't sure if that would be considered patronizing or not. To be safe, I returned his smile, making sure to force it up into my eyes even though the last thing I felt like doing was smiling. "Would you mind looking into the men's dorms to see if you can find him?"

Ethan nodded. "Sure, if it's that important to you."

I trailed after Ethan as he ducked into each men's dormitory.

He came out of the last one with the look of a man who'd dropped a twenty-dollar bill somewhere and couldn't find it. "It doesn't look like he's here." He raised his hands in a shrug. "What did you need? Maybe I can help."

He should help. This was partly his fault. But it wasn't like he would know Jimmy's route. "I don't believe the woman who took the dead man's socks killed him."

Ethan's mouth opened, but I shook my head.

"There's too much that doesn't fit, and I don't think the police have the whole story. I wanted to go look for security cameras along the route where Jimmy went dumpster diving to see if there are any cameras and if they might have caught something. I don't think he died in the train yard. I think he was planted there. I wanted to find Dwayne so he could take me along the route."

Something I couldn't read flickered across Ethan's face. Hopefully it was a touch of guilt for turning Carla in sooner than he promised me.

"That's a lot of *I think*s," he said.

Jerk.

For a second, I thought someone had called him a jerk out loud. Then I realized I'd thought it. It'd been so long since I allowed myself to even think what I really felt if it was negative that I didn't recognize my own thoughts.

Ethan sighed. "But I do owe you. I didn't give you the full time I promised." His gaze swung along the length of the hallway like he didn't want anyone to catch him going along with my craziness. "I can take you. I don't know Jimmy's route, but this is my neighborhood. I collect here. I know every dumpster he might have gone to."

Maybe I shouldn't have called him a jerk—even if only in my head—after all. Not only would his assistance make sure I didn't miss one, but it kept me from having to traipse around the city alone in the dark. "Thank you."

"Don't thank me." The tone of his voice sent a shiver down my arms. "I don't deserve it."

The way he said it made me feel like the jerk. He'd done something wrong, but now he was trying to make it right. I didn't need to rub his mistake in his face.

Instead of saying all that, instead I said, "Your truck or mine?"

Ethan's pickup truck smelled a bit like stale beer and leftover fast food containers. I regretted taking his vehicle as soon as I opened the passenger-side door. If we'd taken my truck, I would have had to pay for the gas, but I would have been a lot more comfortable. As it was, it took all my self-control not to press my scarf over my nose.

"I'll take you along the same route I drive the truck," Ethan said. "That way we won't miss any."

I nodded. My legs felt like I had restless leg syndrome with the way they wouldn't stop jiggling and twitching. My body had been on high alert since I climbed inside.

It was silly. I didn't need to be afraid in this situation. I'm sure a counselor would tell me that I had PTSD and was nervous around men now. Which was true, but also not true. I hadn't been nervous around Jimmy. Or around Dwayne.

Ethan was already driving down the road, and I couldn't think up a good excuse for why I suddenly needed to back out of something so important.

And I shouldn't. If I waited for Dwayne, any tapes on a two-week loop would have taped over any evidence of what happened to Jimmy that night.

Ethan stopped at each dumpster location and patiently waited while I hopped out and scanned the area with the camera feature on my phone.

By three-quarters of the way through the route I remembered from my time with Dwayne and Carla, I'd only found two dumpsters caught on camera.

The owner of the dry cleaner was a woman who looked ten years older than I did. She promised to call the police station and find out who to send her footage to right away. Then it took me another five minutes to get away as she told me how she'd tried to convince other businesses on this street to set up cameras as well to deter crime, but she hadn't had much success.

The second shop was a convenience store. The teenage girl behind the counter had barely looked up from her phone and had told me I'd have to come back the next morning and talk to her manager.

I crawled back into Ethan's truck after my encounter at the convenience store, feeling bone-cold and weary.

Ethan swiveled to face me instead of putting the truck back

into drive. "Maybe we should call it for tonight. Most places are going to be closed soon anyway, and you look tired."

You look tired seemed like one of those things smart men knew better than to say to a woman. In a strange way, though, I appreciated his concern. "I can't stop until we've done the whole route. By tomorrow, any evidence might have been erased."

Ethan got the truck moving again. "My route doesn't go much further."

Neither did Jimmy's regular path. If memory served me, Dwayne and Carla had only taken me to three or four more dumpsters to look for him.

Ethan drove past an alleyway that I remembered. It was wedged between a jewelry store on one side and an accounting firm on the other. I remembered it because Dwayne said the dumpster had an unusual odor to it, and he'd been afraid that he'd find Jimmy decomposing inside.

Now it seemed like one of the most likely places for him to have found something he shouldn't have. Maybe the accounting firm wasn't properly disposing of confidential material, or an employee from the jewelry store had tried to steal something by tossing it into the trash and coming back for it later.

I reached a hand in Ethan's direction, but I didn't actually touch him. "You missed one."

His face twisted into a tight frown. "Are you sure?"

"The alley we just passed has a dumpster at the end. It was one I visited before with Dwayne."

I left Carla's name off.

Ethan slowed the truck down incrementally. "I must be tired, too."

He pulled a U-turn at the next light and turned down the alleyway.

I slid slowly down from his truck. Climbing in and out would have been a lot easier if he'd had running boards. It was a good thing we were almost at the end because my legs felt about as mushy as overcooked spaghetti.

Both the jewelry shop and the accounting firms had doors that opened up into the alley, presumably to provide them with easy access to the dumpster.

The alley wasn't lit by anything more than the moon and the light from my cell phone. I switched over to the camera function.

I held my phone up and turned around, taking my time so that I didn't accidentally miss anything in my fatigue. My eyes felt gritty from squinting at my phone for so long.

The accounting firm didn't seem to have any cameras. I inched around until I faced the jewelry store.

A tiny red pinprick of light glowed from a spot above the door and to the left.

"Any luck?" Ethan said.

I jumped. I hadn't expected him to join me. He'd stayed in the truck at every stop before this.

I turned to face him. He had the hood of his jacket up so that his face was nothing more than a shadow with white puffs of breath coming from the center.

A tingle rushed over my face, making my skin feel strangely hot. He reminded me a little too much of the Grim Reaper.

"Any sign of a camera?" he asked again.

I pocketed my phone. "The jewelry store has one. The storefront was still lit up when we passed before, so hopefully that means we can get them to send the footage to the police tonight."

I went to move past him, but he stepped into my path. "I was hoping you wouldn't find anything."

Ringing filled my ears.

Ethan raised his right arm. He clutched a tire iron in his hand.

CHAPTER 15

The truth slid into place in my mind.

Ethan had his hood up to hide his face in case there was a camera and he needed to dispose of me. He didn't want the camera catching his face.

There was only one reason for him to want to hurt me now, here. He'd killed Jimmy in this alley.

He'd been waiting to see if I found a camera. If I hadn't, he'd have let me move on to the rest of the dumpsters.

It'd been why he tried to pretend this one wasn't here.

Where had Fear's voice been this time when I needed him? Though maybe it was my own fault. I'd been ignoring him so much the past few weeks that he might not be speaking to me anymore.

"I'm really sorry, Isabel." Ethan sounded sincere, but more like someone who'd nicked the bumper of my car rather than like someone who was about to crack me in the skull with a metal pole.

Hadn't he said something about a priest? If he was Catholic, hopefully I could appeal to his sense of right and wrong.

"Killing me to cover up whatever you did isn't going to fix this. You'll never have peace until you confess and turn yourself in."

"I've already been to confession, and I'll go again and do whatever penance the priest tells me to." He gripped his other hand around the trunk of the tire iron. "But I can't let you leave here. I'm safe as long as that video gets erased."

That wasn't the kind of confession I'd meant. I meant confessing to the police. Besides, if my dad had taught me one thing about his faith in God, it was that forgiveness wasn't a free pass to do whatever you wanted.

"I grew up in a Christian home. I know Catholicism is different from Protestant denominations in a lot of ways, but I'm pretty sure that's not how it works. You can't knowingly sin and then say a few Hail Marys to wipe it away."

"What happened to that homeless man was an accident. I didn't know he was in the dumpster when I emptied it into my truck. My priest said it was better for me to do penance for what I'd done by helping others than it was to go to prison for something I didn't mean to do."

"Then why not call the police? If it was really an accident."

Oh, wait. The reek of alcohol in his personal vehicle and his two weeks of sobriety. "Unless you were drinking on the job."

I thought he nodded his head, but it was hard to tell with his bulky hood in place. "The police would have smelled it on me. They'd have made me take a breathalyzer."

And while he wouldn't have gone to prison for accidentally crushing a dumpster diver in his garbage truck if he'd been sober, it became a crime when it happened while he was drunk. His inebriated state might have even meant he ignored safety protocols.

That was why there was beer with Jimmy. It'd been the beer Ethan had with him. If he worked this area regularly, he would have seen that homeless people often hung out at the train yard. It would have been an easy connection for him to make to take Jimmy there and dump him on the tracks, hoping everyone would believe it was an accident.

His plan almost worked, except for the beer. Maybe he assumed Jimmy would have alcohol in his blood. Like Dwayne and Carla had pointed out, people often assumed that all homeless people were also drunks.

Ethan took a step toward me.

I stepped back even though there was nowhere to go. The alleyway ended in a brick wall that was the backside of another building. I could pound on one of the doors, but I might be dead before anyone came. If anyone came.

I moved farther back. If I could reach the dumpster, I might at least find something to defend myself with. "Killing me won't be an accident. What will your priest say to that?"

He lunged for me, tire iron up. "Please forgive me."

I screamed for help and sprinted backward toward the dumpster. Stupid me that I hadn't thought to scream before, but Jarrod used to only beat me harder if I cried out. The instinct to call for help had been beaten out of me, literally.

I tripped over a bag of garbage and careened to the side. I grabbed the bag and heaved it at Ethan.

The dumpster rattled, and a figure launched out of the top. It crashed straight into Ethan.

For a second, I thought I'd fallen into those *Twilight* books that were so popular a few years ago and a vampire had swept down to tackle my attacker. But I was no Bella Swan, and the grunts and oofs said it was two normal men wrestling on the ground.

"This time you gotta be the one to call the police." Dwayne's voice came out in a panting cadence. "I got my hands full."

I spent the three minutes it took the police to reach us trying to figure out whether to give them my real name and risk tipping Jarrod off to which state I was in, giving them my Isabel Addington persona and hoping they didn't run it, or making up a new name entirely and then leaving town the second they finished taking my statement.

Whether it was because of his guilty conscience or because he knew he had no hope of getting away with it anymore, Ethan confessed everything as soon as the police arrived.

He even detailed for them how he'd slashed my tires to scare me away from the mission because I was asking questions and how he reported Carla for having the dead man's socks even though he knew she hadn't killed him.

When he admitted to that last part, Dwayne glanced in my direction.

One officer took Ethan to the station to make his formal confession while the other officer took down our names and phone numbers. I told him my name was Isabel Addington and crossed my fingers that they wouldn't look into her. They shouldn't. The police didn't normally run background checks on witnesses, though if Ethan hadn't confessed, his future lawyer might have.

And, unfortunately, that meant I should also leave the city and move on, whether I wanted to or not. Hopefully, Ethan would sign a confession and it would all be over, but I couldn't take the chance of someone looking too closely at me. If I faded away, changing my phone number, they'd probably assume I was another homeless person who'd disappeared and leave it at that.

The final police officer headed into the jewelry store to get the surveillance footage, leaving Dwayne and me standing in a dark alley. The officer really must have assumed we were both homeless. He hadn't offered to give us a ride.

I held out a hand to Dwayne. Shaking his hand was the only way I could think of to show him respect, to let him know that I appreciated him coming to my rescue even though he thought I'd betrayed them. "Thank you."

He shook my hand, but it was quick, like he was out of practice. "You really hadn't given up on proving Carla didn't do it."

"I really hadn't." I motioned that we should start walking to the mission. The night was only going to get colder. If I told

Lillian what had happened, she might find a spot for Dwayne even though their doors would be closed to clients by now. "What were you doing here?"

He patted his jacket pocket. "I called that lawyer friend of yours. She said if I could find some motive for another person to kill Jimmy, she'd come talk to Carla and see about defending her for free. You had a good idea about searching Jimmy's route, so I figured I'd start on it myself."

This end of Jimmy's route was closest to the police station. That must have been why I hadn't spotted Dwayne at the station or anywhere along the most direct path from the station to the mission. He'd deviated from the path to start investigating reasons Jimmy might have been killed.

"If you call her again," I said, "I'm sure she'll make sure Carla is out before Christmas."

Dwayne slowed his steps. For a second, I wondered if he might be regretting working so hard to get Carla set free because now she'd be back out, bothering him again.

But then he turned his face toward me. "Will you be joining us for Christmas?"

The sooner I left, the sooner I could start establishing myself in a new place. And yet, Christmas seemed like a day that no one should have to spend alone. It seemed like a day that should be spent with people who were happy to see you.

There wouldn't be presents to exchange this year. In fact, if I stayed, I'd spend it volunteering at the mission, giving instead of expecting to receive.

I liked that idea.

"I think I have to stay at least through Christmas. After all, we did just manage to get one of the mission's most avid volunteers arrested. There might not be a Christmas dinner if I go."

LETTER FROM THE AUTHOR

These stories were more "set at Christmas" stories than they were "Christmas stories," but I hope you enjoyed seeing how Nicole and Isabel spent the Christmas after they met.

"Ginger Dead Man" is set before Isabel moves on to Lakeshore, where she has to figure out why someone would kill a hundred-year-old man at his birthday party. If you haven't read *Sugar and Vice* yet, Isabel's story continues there.

Nicole and Mark return to Fair Haven after their aborted honeymoon in "Unsilent Nights." Their story continues in *Rooted in Murder* when Nicole's Great Dane digs up a human bone.

In the meantime, if you like recipes and sneak peaks behind the scenes, make sure you've signed up for my newsletter. I'll be sharing them there soon!

244 | EMILY JAMES

And if you enjoyed this book, I'd really appreciate it if you'd leave an honest review on Amazon or Goodreads. Reviews help fellow readers know if this is a book they might enjoy. Even a short sentence helps!

Love,

Emily

ABOUT THE AUTHOR

Emily James grew up watching TV shows like *Matlock*, *Monk*, and *Murder She Wrote*. (It's pure coincidence that they all begin with an M.) It was no surprise to anyone when she turned into a mystery writer.

Alongside being a writer, she's also a wife, an animal lover, and a new artist. She likes coffee and painting and drinking coffee while painting. She also enjoys cooking. She tries not to do that while painting because, well, you shouldn't eat paint.

Emily and her husband share their home with a blue Great Dane, seven cats (all rescues), and a budgie (who is both the littlest and the loudest).

If you'd like to know as soon as Emily's next mystery releases, please join her newsletter list at www.subscribepage.com/cupcakes.

She also loves hearing from readers.